D1069185

Books for Young Readers by the Author

The Boy Who Went Around the Corner
Lottie's Locket
Miracles on Maple Hill
Plain Girl
(*Newbery Award Winner*)
Curious Missie

Friends
of the Road

Friends
of the Road

VIRGINIA SORENSEN

A MARGARET K. MC ELDERRY BOOK

Atheneum   1978   New York

Map by Anita Karl

Library of Congress Cataloging in Publication Data
Sorensen, Virginia.
Friends of the road.
"A Margaret K. McElderry book."
SUMMARY: Cathy is not looking forward to the
family's tour of duty in Morocco. Then she finds
a wonderful friend.
[1. Morocco—Fiction. 2. Friendship—Fiction]
I. Title.
PZ7.S72Fr   [Fic]   77-17293
ISBN 0-689-50093-9

Copyright © 1978 by Virginia Sorensen
Published simultaneously in Canada by McClelland & Stewart, Ltd.
Manufactured in the United States of America by
Fairfield Graphics, Fairfield, Pennsylvania
Designed by Marjorie Zaum
First Edition

For all the real Tangerines—
Cathy and Ouatif and Raja,
Foxy and Boots,
Lily the Wool Woman,
and the good Doctor.

Friends
of the Road

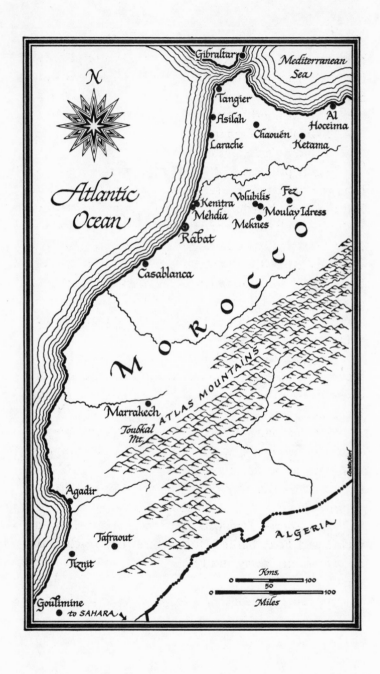

$\mathcal{A}$s the plane skimmed the runway, Cathy saw the huge word TANGER across the top of a scalloped building, the French way of spelling Tangier. Above it was a flowing design—the name written in Arabic. So here they were, in another strange new world.

"I saw Dad!" Tom said.

"You didn't. In all that crowd?"

"I can prove it. He was waving an American flag from the balcony." He sat back, triumphant. As usual. But this time she couldn't care less whether he was first to locate their father or not. What worried her was Foxy. She felt dizzy and her ears were stopped up, as if they were stuffed with cotton. She was sure Foxy's ears felt stopped up too, and he hated strange places and strange people. Whenever she'd had a chance to go up and see him in his box at the front of the plane, he had whined like a baby.

The plane taxied along a runway between fields of blowing green grass. Mom turned her head and spoke excitedly over the high seat. "Look at the flowers, Cathy. Fields of flowers!"

But they had vanished already. The plane stopped. When the engines died Cathy heard Foxy barking. He was bristling so fiercely she could hardly get his leash fastened. All the way down the steps he pulled and slipped.

"See, there's Dad with the flag!" Tom yelled and waved and Foxy barked. Just before they reached the door he pulled away and lifted his leg against a flowering plant.

As usual the officials let Dad come out ahead of

everybody else. In the middle of a kiss, he said to Mom, "I hoped you'd leave Foxy home . . ." and she said, "It was bring him or leave Cathy."

Dad laughed and hugged her. "Well, then! We couldn't do without Cathy, after all!" He introduced a nice young vice-consul named Jerry who took checks for their luggage. Dad threaded a way for them through the crowd. By the time they got to the limousine, right at the door, with flags whipping on the fenders, a Moroccan chauffeur was loading their suitcases. Foxy reared back, growling.

"He's afraid he might have to go with the baggage again," Cathy said. "He barks a lot but he never bites—he just hates strangers."

This didn't seem to make the chauffeur feel any better. But what she meant was that Foxy was just fine when he knew people. In the car she held him, but he insisted on standing by the window, his hair on end. The car swept along a road lined with trees that had been trimmed in the French way so they were huge green balls. Flowering hills lay in every direction.

"Around this next curve you'll see our new town," Dad said. He knew how important first glimpses were; Cathy saw him draw Mom close. And sure enough, there it was, the white Moroccan city. From the plane they had caught one glimpse of it, a mist of white between the mountains and the sea.

Of course, Tom had to bring out his facts: "Tangier is built on seven hills," he said. "Like Rome."

"Our house is white too," Dad said to Mom. Every time they moved to another country he was anxious that their house should please Mom. "Rather like a lacy

4

valentine, I'm afraid, but spacious and new. Really nice."

The hills were really nice, too, Cathy thought. One was a huge carpet of wild gladioli that she longed to get out and pick, but Dad said the cook and housemaid had filled the house with flowers. "You'll love Moroccan markets. Flowers and fruit and vegetables are set out like a fair every day."

Cathy leaned forward over Foxy's head. "Are there any American girls my age? Did you ask?"

"There are some in the American School. They'll be back after Easter holiday." They were temporary, just as she would be. Coming and going, just attending school in Tangier for a while. She sank back in the seat but suddenly Foxy caught sight of a herd of sheep right on the road and leaped to the window, barking his head off.

"Cathy, for heaven's sake!" But Jerry turned around in the front seat to smile. "The last vice-consul here left an old doghouse in his garden," he said. "I'll send it over."

"That's lovely. And I'll have Foxy show you his tricks. They let me walk him in the Madrid airport and he did his tricks for some kids. They thought he was a real show dog." She sat back, stroking Foxy's head, and began to really look at the people along the road and then on the streets of the town. "It looks as if everybody's in *costume!*" she said.

"The ones in red and white with huge hats are Berbers," said Tom the Factotem, as they often called him. "They're the real native people here, like the American Indians at home."

The big car had to slow down for a burro loaded with huge bundles of carrots, among which rode an old man in a ragged brown robe and a blue turban. Mohammed honked and the old man nodded and smiled and gave a leisurely flick with a stick. Along the sidewalk a woman moved briskly, a black sheep trotting beside her. A horseman waited with the traffic at the next corner, and Foxy went wild again, while Cathy gazed, enchanted. "We *never* saw animals in Washington," she said. "Except maybe another dog on a leash."

Two women stood by huge glass doors to welcome them to their new home. Latifa and Zineb, the maid and the cook, were dressed in bright caftans with soft flowered tops and jeweled belts. When Latifa took Cathy to her room, Foxy barked at her all the way. She said something strange to him, the long gold rings in her ears shaking.

"Look, Foxy!" It was the prettiest room Cathy had ever had, with French doors leading onto a terrace all her own. "Your new house will go right there, under that banana tree." But he went into a frenzy of barking at a gardener who had been working in a bed of flowers and now stood up angrily, waving his hoe.

"He'll be okay when he gets used to things," Cathy told Latifa's handsome small son who helped bring in her suitcases. He just smiled, and she had a familiar old feeling of misery; Tangier was like the other places they had lived, where nobody understood a word she said.

After lunch the whole family went to explore every corner of the U.S. Consulate General. Even Foxy went, because every time Cathy left him he howled until she couldn't bear it. It was hard on everyone else, too. Behind the house was a garden with a reflecting pool and a double terrace. Everything seemed double because the office building had glass doors and windows that acted as reflecting mirrors. They seemed to be approaching themselves and Foxy barked at himself barking.

The whole staff, Moroccan and American, had gathered to meet them in Dad's big office on the top floor. Only Jerry was missing until the last minute when he rushed in, his fingers raking his hair into a distracted cockscomb. "That call just went through," he said. "It was *terrible*." He gave Tom and Cathy a flying smile and Foxy a flying pat. "I'll get Foxy's house to you as soon as I've got a minute . . ." and he disappeared.

"Goodness, what was all that?" Mom asked.

"Poor Jerry, half his time is spent trouble-shooting for young Americans." Dad looked a little sick. "He's forever rushing off to the jail or the hospital." Outside again, he told them today's story. "Four college kids drove down from Amsterdam last week, living off the land. One was a Vietnam veteran whose folks gave him a VW van for holidays with his friends. Well—yesterday they gathered mushrooms outside town here and made some soup. And now three of them are dead—yes, including the veteran—and the fellow left alive is raving."

"And poor Jerry had to tell their families?" Mom looked sick too.

Tom said, "They should have had a mushroom book."

"They *had* a book," Dad said. "Jerry found it on the seat of the van." He stopped by the pool and seemed to talk down at the water. "The thing is, in different countries, you should double-check everything. Jerry's just got out a big bulletin for visitors. Why don't you two go right back and read it? *Carefully.*" He leaned down and gave Foxy's ruffled neck a rub. "Foxy, you'd better read this too," he said.

So they went back and found a red-bordered sign posted by the door: *Warnings for All Visiting Americans. Please Read Carefully!!!*

Tom read the first warning and said, "I knew there'd be one about smuggling hash." Then there was one about not eating any mushrooms except those found in the local markets. And then a really scary one about *chewing beads.* "Do not buy native beads for children. Many of them are poisonous if chewed."

What a narrow escape, Cathy thought with a shiver. She always chewed the beads she had on when she was reading.

Then came: "Do not cook like the Moroccans over charcoal braziers, *except in the open.* You can die of asphyxiation." The next warning was the one for Foxy, who for a change was sitting quietly at their feet. "Be careful with pets: be certain they have frequent rabies shots and keep them on a leash in public places."

Cathy stopped reading. Tom went on. "Look at this one," he said. "Do not buy the beautiful birds offered for sale in the markets and on the roadsides. We are trying to stop this inhumane traffic. You can also help to discourage it by *not buying* the attractive cages for sale in the souks."

Cathy was not listening. Was rabies why Dad had told her not to bring Foxy to Morocco? A peculiar long shiver went from her head to her heels. Maybe Foxy should have a booster shot?

Jerry thought a booster shot a good idea and gave them a lift to the Spanish Cathedral. "The Clinic is on that little one-way street, past the carpenters and iron-mongers. You'll see the sign—People's Dispensary for Sick Animals—PDSA. It's run by the British."

The carpenters and ironmongers worked right on the street in front of their tiny workshops. There would be a smell of burning and then a breezeful of fresh cedarwood. The sidewalk was paved with slippery old stones and Foxy walked with his legs stiff and his ears stiffer. When an ugly free-running shorthair tried to come up to him he growled and showed his teeth in a snarl Cathy had never seen on his face before. Walks had always been fun in Washington, owners and dogs circling each other and tangling their leashes. But today Foxy was rigid with distrust and Cathy with a terrible new fear. She knew about rabies. And she knew exactly how Foxy felt about strange places because she felt the same. When words you couldn't understand went flying around you all the time it gave you a helpless, stupid feeling. And of course dog language here was different too. It must be. She gathered the leash close, while Tom drove the strange dog away. They had both noticed an open sore on his side but neither mentioned it. Tom pointed ahead. "There it is, see?" A small sign hung over an arch. *People's Dispensary for Sick Animals*. It was in French and Arabic and then English. *Visitors Welcome.*

Foxy pulled back, sniffing, and Cathy had to drag him along the concrete ramp that led into a cobbled court. It was ringed with stables and small stalls and had a pile of clean fresh hay in the middle. Four donkeys stood in the sun, their backs purple with treated saddle sores. A Moroccan in a white coat and a bright little woolen cap was kneeling by a wretched old horse with one of its hooves in his lap. The horse turned its long melancholy face around to see what was being done to him. Foxy growled like a kettle. The man pointed to a screen door in a building at the front of the compound where a few people and animals waited to see the doctor. Two Moroccan children held armfuls of chickens, whose red-combed perky-pecking heads kept turning about, their eyes glittering with fear. An excited woman held a beautiful white poodle that had, she said, been bitten by a "filthy mongrel." She pushed ahead of the chicken-children, asking for the doctor every time the door opened.

"One moment, please!" They caught a glimpse of a man with a strong round red English face. Cathy liked that face at once, and when they were admitted, along with the two Moroccan children and the poodle-woman, she liked him all over. He was big and solid-looking with absolute kindness in his face and in his hands as he set the poodle up on a white table.

The woman crooned, "Sssssssh, Bitsy darling, it's all right now, here is the doctor," as if the poodle were a child. The doctor opened the dog's bleeding mouth. "Well, when his lip was bitten he must have been doing some snapping of his own," the doctor said mildly.

"A horrid beast rushed up to him—a filthy Moroccan dog."

She was an awful woman, Cathy thought, but she understood her fear and held Foxy more firmly, murmuring to ease his feelings. He had always been upset when they went to a vet.

The doctor told the woman gently that he did not think she needed to worry, but of course, yes, as she said, she must make sure. Then he turned to a man sitting quietly in a corner, with a little gibbon in his lap. The monkey's ear was infected. It cried like a baby while he probed away with a cotton swab. His assistants took care of the chickens, giving them shots in their thighs covered with golden brown feathers; the children watched with anxious eyes. Outside, suddenly, came the cry of a donkey, which sounded for all the world like a desperate cry for help. Tom looked out of the door, grinning. "You know," he said, "donkeys sound exactly like those peacocks we used to hear in Bangkok in the early morning. Remember?"

Donkeys and peacocks. But Tom's odd comparison seemed natural here. The doctor smiled and held out his hand. "You're our new American consulate family," he said. And to Cathy, "I've heard about you. Your dad says you like animals better than people. Is that so? I told him that sometimes so do I." Foxy wriggled with pleasure when the doctor rubbed around his ears and asked his name. Cathy, not looking while Foxy got a shot, saw something marvelous moving on top of a high shelf of books. An *owl?*

"That's Little Owl," the doctor said, following her eyes. "We rescued him the other day, half starved, but he's doing nicely now. I was just going to feed him and weigh him in; like to watch?"

The assistant climbed up a ladder to bring Little Owl down perched on his finger. "This is Mustapha," the doctor said. "He speaks six people-languages and all the languages of all the animals besides." Obviously Mustapha was now speaking "owl" to the bundle of brown and white fluff fastened to his finger. Delicately he moved his hand toward what must be the tiniest scale in the world. "He lost a quarter ounce yesterday," the doctor said. "Good—he's got it back now. Let's see if he has his appetite back as well."

Little Owl's huge jewel eyes gazed unblinking, but his feathers fluffed nervously as he was lifted from the tiny brass bowl of the scales onto a perch. Dr. Prescot got a small tweezer out of a cupboard, and Mustapha brought a dishful of tiny cubes of red meat. When Little Owl was offered a piece he opened his mouth wide and the doctor pushed the food in exactly the way mother birds do. Gently. Not hurrying, his face intent and concerned.

Presently, while Little Owl ate, he glanced at Cathy and said, "You were lucky you could bring your dog along. You'd have been pretty lonely without him, I imagine. I was glad to hear he had come, and so was everybody else."

Everybody else? Cathy looked surprised and he began to laugh. "There are not so many of us Anglos and Americans here," he said. "We're apt to know all the news about each other."

Little Owl gulped the last piece down. "There you are!" and the doctor deposited him on Mustapha's finger again. "Up you go!" Then he said, "Want to weigh Foxy while you're here? It's good to keep track. Sometimes in a new place we get off our feed a bit—eh, Foxy?" Foxy hated scales and tubs about equally, but this time he sat quiet as the doctor's finger moved around his ears.

Outside again, Cathy said, "I wish I had a dad like Dr. Prescot. He really loves animals, doesn't he?"

Tom stopped short. "What a dumb thing to say. Dad likes animals all right. They're just not his special line, that's all." His voice sounded angry, but ashamed too, as if he might have had the same thought himself.

At home they found Jerry had already sent the dog-house. Latifa's son had got over some of his shyness. He spoke French, it turned out and so did Cathy. His name was Abdulatif, and he was to help clean the house for Foxy. As they brushed and cleaned it together under the banana tree, Cathy learned with interest that in Spanish dog was *el perro,* and here in Morocco something that sounded like *zherro.*

Gravely, Abdulatif said, "I am speaking Espanol y Français y Arab only." He would like now to learn English and go with her and Tom to the American School on Avenue Christopher Colombo.

"Dear Carol," Cathy wrote to her best friend in Washington.

I am writing late at night. I can't seem to get to sleep. Foxy keeps making a fuss. He hates his new house even though I put his old quilt in it. I think one of the troubles here is all the strange noises. People keep going by on the road and awhile ago

13

there was a whole bunch with flutes and drums, awfully loud, that sounded like pipes. There's a guard marching around and around the consulate all day and all night. Dad says every consulate has to have guards now because of all the shootings and kidnappings and places getting blown up. There's a wind tonight that really whistles and the palm trees and a huge banana tree just outside my window make the hugest rustling you can imagine. Latifa, our maid, told Mom she can tell the weather by the direction of the wind. A west wind means good weather and an east wind means bad. Or maybe it's the other way about; I'll have to ask her again. She says there's almost always a wind in Tangier, from one direction or the other. Tom says the Straits of Gilbraltar, where the Mediterranean goes into the Atlantic, make a kind of tunnel for the wind to blow through.

Another strange sound is the big voices from the minarets. A sort of priest chants from these tall towers five times a day, calling people to say their prayers.

I'm learning lots of new things I'll write to you about. If you keep my letters the way you did when I was in Bangkok I can use them again for school. I haven't got to the post office yet to see if there are any nice stamps for your collection. Dad says he thinks there are some special issues of flowers and birds, but mostly the stamps are of the king in different colors.

Foxy just yipped again. Maybe the shot he got today is bothering him. Or maybe it's all the other dogs barking. I've never heard so many dogs barking in the night.

At that point, Dad called, "Cathy! Turn off that light and get to sleep. And can't you shut that dog *up?*"

She lay half asleep in the dark for a long time, aware of the strange world around her. Foxy was still now, but the wind blew and blew.

Suddenly she was fully awake. Gunfire? She must be dreaming. But there it was again. Close. And somebody was running down the hall—Dad shouting something to Mom. When Cathy opened her door Mom was yelling, "Ward, don't go out till you're sure what it is—"

But he was gone. When Cathy joined Mom at the big front windows he was talking to the guardian at the front gate. It swung open and the guard ran in, waving his arms and his gun. They talked together, excitedly, and then Dad turned and came back to the house.

"Only some police after stray dogs," he said. "Because of that rabies scare. Better keep Foxy on his leash, Cathy."

She had left the big French doors of her bedroom open and she called to Foxy as she went back in. He didn't come. When she went onto the terrace she saw at once what he had been doing. He had dug a hole under the garden fence. She ran around the outside of the house, calling his name frantically. Dad and Mom were talking to the guard. "I can't find Foxy."

They knew something, she could tell. Dad put a hand on her shoulder. "Cathy, I warned you, remember?" and when she headed for the gate he called, "Cathy, stay here!" but she went right on running. Just outside the gate stood a jeep with a trailer behind it. In the seat was a policeman with a gun across his arm. As she passed she saw something horrible. In the trailer lay a pile of dogs, tangled together, flung in like a heap of garbage.

A few yards down the hill a crowd of people had begun to gather. Foxy lay near them, beside the road. She knelt over him and he lifted his head. He was still alive then. All the people seemed to be talking at once. She heard somebody saying "Petite Americaine" and "the Consul-General" as she gathered Foxy up. He looked at her, his head wobbly and his body limp and heavy. But there was no blood. She carried him to the gate where Mom stood, looking sick. "Cathy, the police say Foxy was running on the road. They had orders to shoot every stray."

But Cathy, with one glance at the horrible jeep, began yelling. "They could see he had a collar on! This is *Foxy!*"

She had to get him to Dr. Prescot. At once. Where was Mohammed with the car? Dad protested, "It's no use, Cathy." But Mom said, "If we don't try, she'll never forgive us."

Mohammed came running, pulling on his coat. Latifa carried a coat for Cathy and put it around her shoulders as she and Mom got into the car.

"Not that way," Cathy cried as the car rushed past the street near the cathedral. But it was a one way street and Mohammed had to drive all the way to the big square in the middle of the town to get back to the clinic. Stumbling over the rough stones in the arched passage, Cathy saw Mustapha opening a door. Without a word he took Foxy from her very carefully and laid him once more on the white table. If only Foxy would object the way he had before, Cathy thought, but he only lay quietly, looking up at her. Mustapha murmured some strange answer to the frightful panting. And to Cathy, "Soon the Doctor comes."

She thought, "If only he would wag his tail . . ."

Mustapha's face was brown and kind, and it was a relief that he didn't look worried, only absorbed as if (like Foxy sometimes) he heard something she could not hear. The door opened. No, not the doctor yet. The other Arab assistant. They both stood over Foxy, speaking together in their mysterious Moorish tongue. She felt as if she were listening all over, not for words, which were hopeless to understand, but for the sound of doom—or for a blessing. Foxy was breathing, after all. His eyes rolled. She reached out and scratched him around his ears, as he loved her to do, so he would know she was there.

Mom put her arm around Cathy's shoulder. It was soft with the fur of her jacket. Cathy had hated that jacket ever since she had joined a save-the-animals group in Washington and written a piece for the school magazine: "The Fur Trade Like the Slave Trade MUST END!" She began to shiver uncontrollably. Then the door opened. The strong feeling of the doctor filled the room.

"Well, well, what has happened to Foxy?" Mustapha took his rough brown coat from him and handed him a white jacket. And at once Cathy felt better. This was the person who knew, who would say, who really cared. Her eyes followed his, easier now, looking at Foxy's eyes, at his mouth—both very white—and at his paper white tongue.

"He was shot running away. That's the usual thing." There were wounds on his hind legs and his back, hardly any blood. The bare skin between his legs was ghost white too. The doctor's eyes moved to Cathy's face and over her head to Mom and back again. "He's bleeding badly inside from the shots," he said gently. "What a fright he had—poor fellow." His strong hand stroked Foxy's throat. "His legs suddenly stopped working, you see. I'm afraid he is paralyzed."

"So . . ." Cathy swallowed. She could not say, "So he can never run," let alone, "So he will die."

"Perhaps an hour. Perhaps not so long," the doctor said. "I could help him sleep now. Sooner."

Cathy felt Mom's hand close over hers. She had to decide. She stood without speaking, looking at Foxy, and then nodded and turned away. The thought came: yes, help him to sleep soon, oh yes, I don't want him hurting any more.

"Mustapha—" Dr. Prescot said.

She stood outside in the passage under the arch. She could not stop shivering and leaned against the wall. The policeman came from the street and went in to speak to the doctor. Mom said, "I suppose he was only following orders." After all, that is what policemen must always do. But when he and Dr. Prescot came out, Cathy could hardly bear to look at him.

Mom said, "Tell the officer I appreciate his concern."

"I'm afraid it's not so much concern about Foxy," Dr. Prescot said. "He has to take a body back for every cartridge he fires—or else he has to pay—"

Cathy could speak again then because she had to: "But I'm taking Foxy home!"

They took him, wrapped in a clean sack, and Cathy did not look at the policeman or at any of the crowd now gathered outside in the street. Dr. Prescot said there was a cemetery for pets in Tangier, kept by the PDSA out on the mountain road. "People need a place to bury their pets."

But Cathy told him, "I'll put Foxy in the garden. Where his house is."

The doctor came with them to the car. "These mistakes happen everywhere," he said. "In countries where there are many poor, people can't afford to feed their pets, so they let them out at night to forage. When they become a danger, the police must do the best they can."

When they got back to the consulate, Tom was waiting out on the road. He might be a terrible tease, but he always helped when he was really needed. In the garden, he did most of the digging. Mom came out and said, "Maybe we should have taken Dr. Prescot's offer. Foxy liked to be with other dogs, remember."

Mom didn't usually say anything that silly. Foxy liked *being*. And now he wasn't. Cathy looked at her and turned away; Tom didn't give her a glance. When she had gone in he said, "He was the smartest dog I ever saw. The way he could sit up and speak and play the piano—"

"The only thing I could never get him to learn was to wipe his feet on the mat."

Tom said, "They always use fox terriers for show dogs. He could have been a show dog." This had been said hundreds of times, but it had to be said once more. They wrapped Foxy in his old quilt and covered him over. Cathy thought, I never want another pet as long as I live. Foxy was the best pet in the world.

The next morning the big packing boxes, with the family belongings, were delivered. Usually it was fun to see things again, the special things Cathy had carried to England and Belgium and Bangkok and back and forth to Washington. She set up the rack for her records but didn't particularly want to listen to anything. In a room with so many window-doors there wasn't much space for posters. She spread them on her bed, the one for peace, and the jungly one with birds and animals that said *SAVE OUR WORLD*. At the bottom of the box was her ancient old Pooh Bear, huge and limp. She remembered Mom carrying him in airports when she was too little to carry him herself.

Tom was late for lunch. He had begun exploring on his bike the minute it was unpacked. *He* could go out all he wanted, she thought, but if she went alone everybody would have a fit. "After all, he's older and he's a boy," they always said.

At the luncheon table, Mom said to Dad, "Tom's got to be told to mind what I say. I *told* him to be back on time and to take Cathy—"

"I didn't *want* to go," Cathy said. What she really hated was having them insist Tom take her along whether he wanted to or not. She didn't like going with him anyway; he never stopped to look at things, just whizzed along.

"You'd rather sit around by yourself." A familiar

worried look was exchanged between Mom and Dad. "Cathy, you really can't just sit around and *brood*."

What they don't seem to know, Cathy thought, lowering her head over her plate, is that I'm not brooding. *I'm in mourning.*

"We've been discussing it," Dad said in his bright-*bright* voice, "and we think we should get you another dog right away. A *big* dog this time. Then you could go around on your own."

"I don't want another dog," she said. "And I don't *like* big dogs, I like little dogs." She had liked Foxy. Some bread stuck where her throat swelled shut.

"Really, Cathy," Dad said, with the bright note beginning to harden, "you must try to be reasonable. I warned you before you came, remember, that Foxy shouldn't come."

She nodded without speaking. Why must he keep reminding her that it was all her own fault?

Tom rushed in. He had met some guys who went to the American School. There was this Bicycle Club—Mom gave him a withering look, and he said, "Cathy, we passed this *great* stable. They're having a big horse show in June."

"I hope they don't have those wild Arabians," Mom said.

"They won't have any horses the champ can't handle," Tom said.

Cathy hated him to call her "the champ." There hadn't been anybody at that riding school in Washington to compete with. A bunch of babies. "If I had a horse of my own . . ." she thought. All her life she had wanted a horse of her own. But they never stayed in one place long enough. In Bangkok there had been a marvelous pony called Shakri, but just as she got him so he understood every word, every move, she had to leave. Every time she got a pet or a friend, up and away, up and away. . . .

"They do have wonderful horses here in Morocco," Dad was saying. "Jerry told me that on the King's birthday hundreds of horses marched in the parade. He said the discipline was fantastic."

"When we go on a trip," Mom said, "we must see that famous Arabian Fantasia. The riders spur their horses and stop suddenly, firing their guns. I saw it once in a film."

"There's a painting of it in the Consulate," Dad said. "Cathy, you must go over today and see it."

Latifa came in with a hot dish to serve Tom.

"Cathy, you haven't eaten a *thing*," Mom said.

"I'm not hungry."

"But you'll love the dessert. Strawberries."

"I had them last night. If I eat them every day I break out. You know that. If I eat more now I'll have hives all around my belt."

"That's just *nerves*," Mom said.

"Or fleas," Tom said. "They're all over the place here."

Mom looked at him, pained. Fleas would only remind Cathy of Foxy.

Cathy got up. "Excuse me, please," she said.

"Why don't you take a nap?" Mom called after her. And to Dad, "She's been awake since before dawn. I heard her."

"Nobody can sleep after dawn in this place," Tom

said. "All those guys moaning from the mosques."

Cathy rather liked the chanting voices, she thought, closing her door. Nobody could mind being wakened by such beautiful sounds, if there was anything to be wakened *for*. One thing she really must hang on her wall was an embroidered picture, a sort of sampler that her grandma had made when she was a little girl. In Washington she had hung it opposite her bed so she saw it first thing in the morning. It was a quotation from the Bible—THIS IS THE DAY THE LORD HATH MADE, WE WILL REJOICE AND BE GLAD IN IT.

How could she be glad in this day? She lay on her face, holding the pillow tight until she could no longer breathe. You could smother yourself in a pillow. But her heart began beating wildly and she turned over, frightened, and got up to find the sampler and some tape with which to put it up.

Over their coffee, Mom was saying to Dad, "I should have stayed in Washington with Cathy until the end of school. It was a mistake, dragging her to another new place at midyear."

"We decided only after lots of discussion." He stirred at his coffee impatiently, the way he always did when he was nervous.

She replied crossly, "You shouldn't use so much sugar."

"You should see what the Moroccans use!"

She let that go, but said, "We had a lot of discussion about bringing Foxy too. What a mistake *that* turned out to be."

"That wasn't *my* mistake." He stood up, ready to

go back to the office where quite often international problems seemed much easier to deal with than domestic ones.

"I *did* hope there might be some girls her age here," Mom said.

"There will be, as soon as Easter holidays are over." He started for the door, turned and said, "She's always all right when she's settled in school."

Tom's bicycle scattered gravel out front. Off again. "Too bad she's not like Tom. He's so open and easy. He finds friends right away wherever we go."

"They're just different animals, that's all," Dad said. "Please try to remember what Dr. Armstrong said— *Cathy likes to be alone.*"

She watched him disappear beyond the terrace. She could never believe a broody child liked to be alone. A loner to her meant "unpopular," "unhealthy," "too much reading and not enough activity." Awful that this Foxy thing had to happen just before Cathy's birthday. Last year there had been a wonderful party. All of Cathy's classmates at that good Washington school had come. Now Cathy would remember how Foxy had sat at the table and done all his tricks. She agreed with Ward that another dog was probably the answer, but a really *good* dog. The French consul's wife said a poodle could be flown down from Paris, her husband could arrange it. Poodles were bright and teachable.

The phone rang. Dad said, "I just had a call from Kent, the British Consul-General. His daughter is here for her spring holidays, and she's just Cathy's age. He said his wife would call you about getting them together."

The moment she hung up, the phone went again. "For tea? We'd love to come."

Cathy wailed when she heard. "Oh, Mom—*tea.*"

"They have a girl your age. And her mother says they know some Moroccan girls. Maybe we'll have a birthday party yet!"

"I don't want a birthday," Cathy said.

"Please don't be silly," Mom said. "People have birthdays whether they want them or not."

Foxy had been a birthday present, Cathy thought as she turned away. We celebrated his birthday with mine.

"Take a shower and put on the pretty blue dress," Mom called after Cathy.

"Is it *today?*"

"She only has two weeks before she goes back to school. We thought the sooner the better."

"She s going away in two weeks? Why do I have to meet her then? English kids are always so *snooty.*" She knew Mom hated it when she whined. "Even if I should happen to like her, she'll just go away."

"Please, dear. *Try,*" Mom said.

She always said that. Cathy turned the shower on hard and fast. Please dear, *try.* Please dear, *try.* Everywhere they went there were these nasty kids of these different consuls Dad called his "opposite numbers." They were always older, looking down at you, or younger and being stupid. And all that clip-clip Lady British talk. She knew exactly what this girl was going to be like.

A little later they sat side by side eating thin white sandwiches without any crusts. She looked okay, Cathy thought, and she had a nice name. Pippa. Pippa. Like a bird chirping. But they were edgy, both of them, like two suspicious cats. After eating some cake, Pippa's mother said, "Perhaps, Pippa dear, you would like to show Cathy the view from your room."

They walked stiffly up a wide staircase. Cathy liked huge old houses like this one, with high ceilings and chandeliers dripping prisms. Nothing Valentine about this. Everywhere, British embassies and consulates looked imposing, really as if, she thought, they were built for the Queen herself to live in. There was always a portrait of her, in white satin and jewels and ribbons, looking like the mistress of the house.

Pippa's room was cheerful with a splendid view over a wide terrace and flowering garden. Beyond was an interesting Moroccan cemetery with graves looking like white coffins on top of the ground. A high white bell tower stood just beyond, and right next to it was a minaret with colorful designs. "The bell tower is our Anglican church, St. Andrews," Pippa said politely. "It's very old. The early English here were clever to build their church in the Moslem style, don't you think? The altar is a Moroccan arch with the Lord's Prayer around it *in Arabic*."

Cathy leaned on the sill, looking, and thinking, yes, she's one of the real smarty-smarts explaining about art and architecture because she thinks Americans are dumb. She said, extra politely, "There's a minaret at the bottom of the hill below our consulate. I hear the priests chanting in the night."

"This is so close the voices are very loud, you can imagine," Pippa said. "Once the voice of the muezzin

came at the same moment St. Andrew's bell was ringing . . ." And just then, as if by magic, the big voice
began to chant from the bright tower.

They looked at each other. Just as they were talking about it! Pippa asked, "Have you ever wondered
whether these chantings mean the same thing to Moroccan children as our church bells mean to us? The people
here pray five times a day," she added. "You see them
along the roads, in doorways, wherever they happen to
be when the time comes. They put their foreheads on
the ground."

For a moment they stood silent. "There's an absolutely super place I can go to watch people," Pippa
said, "and nobody knows where I am." It was as if she
held her breath, wondering whether Cathy could be
trusted with a secret. Then she suddenly plunged: "You
see that fir tree at the top of the garden by the wall? Just
there." It was an old tree, gnarled and mostly lying in
one direction because of the winds from the sea. "I'll
show you the big flat branch. I can lie there for ages and
look at everything on the other side of the wall. And at
everybody."

They stood quiet again, listening. Beyond the
towers and the swarming old town lay the blue sea.
Today the air was so sharp and clear they could see the
outline of Gibraltar and the white cities along the coast
of Spain.

"I love strange places," Pippa said. *"Foreign* places.
It's lucky to be like that, Mum says, if you happen to be
a Foreign Service Child."

"We say 'State Department Brat,' " Cathy said.

Their eyes met. And suddenly, amazingly, Pippa's eyes filled with tears and she burst out, "I've felt so frightfully sad I could hardly bear it!" she said. "Dr. Prescot told me about your little dog."

"Dear Carol, I have a friend here already."

There the letter had stopped. What on earth could you even start saying about the way Pippa was? They were the same age and within two inches and three pounds of each other. If you said it in metres and kilos it made them seem even closer. They loved dogs and had told each other about every one they had ever had. They loved cats, too, and their dignity, as if they were afraid of being absurd. Birds, but not caged, wild through binoculars. And especially horses. "Tomorrow morning," Pippa had said when they parted the first time, "we'll pick you up and take you to the stables." How could you tell Carol about that, about how gorgeous the horses were, and the trails; it would seem as if she liked it better here than riding with Carol in Rock Creek Park. Anyway, there wasn't time to write more just now. She'd do it later, when Pippa had gone back to school.

Impossible, just yet, to think abut Pippa going. But in July she would be back and then they would have the whole summer together, every day. They talked so fast and excitedly when they were together that they got full of wind and began to belch. Which made them fall down laughing.

The best part, the most incredible, was that they had the same future plans. They wanted to be veterinarians. Cathy said, "Tom says it's *nuts* for women to be vets. He said, 'What about *bulls?*' And good old Mom said, 'They'll all love Cathy so much they'll lie down like Ferdinands.' "

Tom had been right about how good the horses were at the stables on Mountain Road. Especially the two horses that seemed to be the same sort of friends she and Pippa were themselves. Pippa had been riding her horse during every holiday for a year. "His name is Tarik, which means somebody very handsome," she said. "The only other one I wanted to ride was his pal Habibi—in Arabic that means *My Own True Love*. Nobody except the riding master ever rode Habibi along with me and Tarik."

"Why are you so sure I can manage him?" Cathy asked.

"I don't know why, but I just am. Naturally. You're the right sort, that's all." Pippa had been pleased when she was proved to be right.

Now and then, smelling the good stable smells again, lifting the familiar weight of a saddle, Cathy would think, I shouldn't be this happy again *so soon*. But here was Pippa, mounted beside her and shouting as she rode off, "Now I'll show you my favorite trail!"

Soon off the paved Mountain Road, they forded a spring stream and plunged, loping, into meadows. There was the Pet Cemetery with rows of small square headstones. Beyond was the Rest Home where Dr. Prescot's PDSA kept tired and sick old horses and donkeys. Pippa fed sugar to her favorite two, old Brandy and Soda, who had been sandhorses all their hard lives but now grazed on lush grass and slept in a barn out of the rain. The Moroccan in charge was a kindly old man named Allal, who somehow seemed to be resting after a hard life, too. He had his own flock of sheep, and Pippa said he could call it together with a flute he had made from a bit of bamboo.

The whole countryside was wild with spring, every field a carpet of flowers. Daisies that Pippa called marguerites. Myrtle that Pippa called periwinkles. Brilliant red cloverblooms sprinkled rubies among the grass. Allal gathered a bunch of gladioli and they hung them like necklaces on the horses. As they waited to cross the Mountain Road again, two busloads of tourists waved at them.

"Can't you imagine them saying, 'Look at the natives!' "

"Tourists think when they've been riding around a place for a day they've *been* there." Pippa's contempt reminded Cathy of Tom.

"You know what Tom heard a dumb American tourist say? 'Look, they've still got their Christmas decorations up!' He really withered her. 'Red and green just happen to be the Moroccan national colors,' he said, 'and Moroccans just happen to be Moslem and not Christian, and their green symbolic star doesn't happen to be the one the Wise men followed on Christmas Eve.' "

"Good for him," Pippa said. "He should see some of the British tourists going round the bazaars looking superior."

At that moment nobody had ever felt more superior than they did themselves, loping side by side. They passed the golf course and followed a rising path. Pippa said there was a place with the biggest view of any, every direction. Easy riding would take them there in half an hour. New pine buds burned like candles in the sun. The sharp healing smell of eucalyptus came from brown leaves on the ground and from long green leaves on the trees above their heads. Up and up they rode, through glittering air, until suddenly, far below, they saw the sea. Behind them, glimpses of the white city; south, the high peaks of the Rif, north, the Straits of Gibraltar and the Rock of Gibraltar itself, and west the Atlantic, going on forever.

They rested with the horses. "Isn't it odd," Pippa said, "when you look over a country like this, you start feeling it belongs to you?"

To *us*, Cathy thought, with a deep, wide happiness unlike anything she had ever felt before.

"This summer we can swim sometimes on the beaches in town and sometimes on the Atlantic side by the Caves of Hercules. Imagine, you haven't even seen the caves yet! You can see where people in the ancient days cut out their millstones."

"I'll wait and see them with you, when you come back."

"Hercules' wife was Tingit—they say that was Tangier's ancient name. Have you heard the story of how Hercules and Antaeus fought for her? It's a very symbolic story. Hercules had to lift Antaeus into the air before he could win, because Antaeus got all his power and strength from the earth."

On the way back they saw a herd of sheep and a young shepherd in a ragged brown robe; he carried a long crooked stick and looked exactly like a picture from the Bible. "Look, Pippa, a baby lamb!" The shepherd smiled and waved when they stopped, pointing. He picked the lamb up and brought it for them to see. But suddenly its mother came bleating and anxious and before they so much as touched its soft wool he let it go.

"Did you notice," Cathy said, "it had *golden eyes?*"

"And not round pupils—sort of square—did you see?"

"If only we could have held him."

They circled through hills golden with sedge and mimosa, rode along meadows pink with asphodel. Along the road children held out bouquets for sale and Berber women walked, bent double under huge bundles of sticks. One woman, in a bright red and white skirt with a baby on her back, offered eggs from a basket, another goat cheese on a fan of palm.

"When I first came here, I thought everybody was in costume," Pippa said.

"So did I!"

Small thatched houses had high fences of prickly pear. "When the fruit is ripe on them they're like purple figs with needles," Pippa said.

"I know. Tom read about them—they're called Barbary Figs because of the Berbers. But Christopher Columbus brought the first ones to Spain from the West Indies."

"And they wandered over here? Imagine, from America to Europe to Africa." It seemed marvelous to them that plants could be wanderers like people, traveling and settling down all over the world.

At the stables again they had no need to speak. Cathy knew already how Habibi had come by his name. He was not only a nuzzling horse like some others she had known, but he was actually a *kissing* horse. He moved his big tender lips over her arms and her neck and even her cheeks. He loved it when she was watering him and riffled the water with her fingers so close he could snuffle at them.

"What if you had arrived after I'd gone back to school!" Pippa said, aghast at the awful thought.

"But I didn't. I came *now*." So it was all meant to be. Fate. For sure. Forever.

Now there would really be a party, a party with a reason for being, the kind Mom loved to give. She had found through the headmaster of the American School three Moroccan girls who would be in Cathy's class. From a PX at Kenitra, the U.S. army base near Rabat, she and Dad brought prizes for games and a fishpond, and a complete packet of party decorations.

"It's childish, actually," Cathy said. "But that's my Mom, the living American Way."

Having said it, she and Pippa madly enjoyed themselves. The morning of the party they decorated the terrace with flags and bunting and paper ribbons and stars swinging on strings. Instead of place cards they printed names with poster paint on a huge paper tablecloth. On a big sheet hung in a corner for the fishpond they pinned paper fish and sailboats.

Abdulatif hung around to watch, and they heard Tom teasing him in his sort of fractured French. "No for *you*. It's a party for *girls*." But when it was almost time for the guests to arrive, Abdulatif appeared in his best clothes, with a very white shirt and a tie, with Latifa beaming behind him. He carried a gift wrapped in bright flowered paper.

"Is he going to stay?" Cathy asked. "He's only eight."

Mom gave her a familiar, "Please, Cathy" look. What could she do, considering the present and all? "Latifa is so anxious for him to learn English," she said, "and I've promised to help him."

The bell rang and there were two more eight-year-olds, the twin daughters of the French Consul, Poupette and Lisette. Pippa whispered, "They're at least good for practicing our French."

Then came two pretty, shy Moroccan girls, Najat and Ouatif, and an older American named Karen whose father was with the Voice of America.

"Now everybody is here except the girl called Rajah," Mom said, "but I think we can begin. What shall we have first, Musical Chairs or the Fishpond?" Nobody said anything for a long awkward minute. Cathy wished Mom wouldn't put on her school-teacher-ish voice when she managed a party. "Shall we be democratic and have a voice vote? Those for Musical Chairs . . . " But they had all begun to vote at once, until it sounded like Musical Fish and Chairs in a Pond. Abdulatif imitated Cathy so it was five to three for Musical Chairs.

"Set up eight chairs—put their backs together—by the time we're ready Rajah will probably be here."

But she was not. And they took one chair away and Mom started a record. But Abdulatif had disappeared.

"Maybe he decided not to play because Tom teased him about being the only boy," Cathy was saying, just as he came back from the kitchen with his mother.

"Abdulatif says he saw Rajah come to the gate with her father," Latifa said. "At three o'clock. But then she went—again away . . ."

"Why?" Mom asked.

Abdulatif stood looking at his shiny shoes, not having enough English to answer. "He says . . ." Latifa came close to Mom and spoke in a low voice.

Mom went red. "Oh, dear . . . I'm so sorry. Cathy, she must have seen the others with gifts, Latifa says. She thinks Rajah didn't understand." Her expression was familiar. When you were new in these strange countries it was hard to do things right. She told them to begin the game and started the music again, looking worried. They marched around and around, the young ones terribly serious and Ouatif and Najat giggling like Cathy and Pippa as if they couldn't care less. But when the music stopped they all scrambled for places. Poor Abdulatif was the one who found himself without a place. Everybody laughed and one chair was taken away and the music began again. Abdulatif joined the parade and everybody stopped. "No, you're out, Abdulatif—you're *out!*"

He looked stricken. What had he done that was wrong? Maybe, Cathy thought, he thinks we have put him out because he's a boy, just as Tom said. "You can play next time!" she called to him but could see he didn't understand.

"Never mind, he'll get the point in a minute," Pippa said. And when the music stopped again and

Ouatif stood by him, also banished, panting and laughing, and another chair was taken away and the music began again, he smiled once more.

Cathy knew it was babyish of her, but whenever she played in a game she really wanted to win. Finally there was only Pippa marching around with her and she knew that Pippa didn't care a fig for winning, but she *really did*. That Washington psychiatrist had said it was because Tom had won everything they ever played together from the time she was born.

The music stopped again, and she edged into the chair under Pippa, sliding in like a fish.

Mom called, "A tie!"

"No, it isn't. I'm sitting, Pippa isn't!"

"I'm sitting on your lap!" and suddenly it was the funniest thing that ever happened and they collapsed off the chair. Somebody said, "Here comes Rajah."

Rajah was walking across the terrace with careful steps, her black eyes fixed ahead of her. Beside her came her father, a handsome Moroccan with a fine striped woolen robe and a red fez on his head. But Cathy and Pippa forgot to speak to either one when they saw what Rajah was carrying. A tiny lamb, all white except for its delicate nose and standout ears which were as coal black as its long bony legs to the knees.

They rushed for him together, but Rajah's father stepped forward and held out a hand. He spoke to Mom in French. "I have come with my daughter. There must be first the permission. An animal is a great care; it eats very much."

Cathy cried, "But Mom—*of course!*"

And Mom said, "How very kind—"

Rajah smiled, pleased with the excitement she had brought with her. Cathy held out her arms and carefully, ritually, the lamb was given. She stood holding this incredible, this marvelous creature in her arms.

Latifa looked horrified. She moved swiftly to Mom and said, "It is sick. You see how small. It will surely die." A sickly little lamb that had been taken from its mother would become another tragedy too soon after the little dog.

Pippa said, "Oh, Cathy—he looks as if he had boots on!" And together they said, "That's his name. He's *Boots!*"

Everybody stood around in a circle, cooing like doves.

Rajah said, "I am sorry to be late. But the lamb must be made clean, my mother said, for bringing."

Cathy said, awed, "He's the best pet I ever had," and saw Pippa's face and said, "He's *ours*, isn't he? You'll help me take care of him."

Suddenly he lifted his head and made a sound, a trembling little bleat. He agreed. He was theirs.

"But surely," Mom said to Rajah's father, "he is too young to be without his mother."

He shook his head. "His mother was killed yesterday on the road. Rajah had heard of *le petit chien* . . ." He looked at Cathy who was sitting herself gently down with the lamb on her lap and lowered his voice. "We have shame for this." Her dog had died and therefore she was given another living thing. Cathy looked up; everybody nodded, understanding. Pleased.

37

"Mom, I *can* keep him, can't I?"

"He is very young," Mom said helplessly. "Without a mother—"

"But I'll be his mother now!"

"He'll have two of us," Pippa said, "and Dr. Prescot will tell us exactly what to do."

Rajah stood beaming and her father bowed himself out.

"Now the fishpond," Mom said.

"Let me hold him for a minute," Pippa said.

"His eyes *are* golden—see?" Now they could look as long as need be. "Rectangles. The pupils—golden rectangles."

After the fishpond the birthday cake was brought blazing from the kitchen. Cathy blew the candles out with one breath and said, "Pippa, we can get a basket at that place in the Socco."

"Dr. Prescot will know where to get a bottle and nipples."

"Shall we see if he likes ice cream?" But he leaped back at the cold on his nose.

"Cathy, now it's time to open all the presents," Mom said. Pippa held Boots while everybody else crowded around to see the packages opened, one by one. There was a feeling of anti-climax, the best had been seen already. Mom fussed enough for two: "Lovely! Put it on, Cathy!" over a blouse with delicate embroidery and buttons all down the front. "What wonderful leather!" over a purse and a small camel with a rider dressed like a sheik. "Latifa, Abdulatif, it is too much—" as she hung on Cathy's neck a string of incredibly huge amber beads. Pippa had brought a Moroccan harness woven of thick twisted threads with long fringes and tassels in bright colors wound with gold.

"I'll keep all these things forever," Cathy said. "I'll take them everywhere I ever go."

But the lamb was *now*. Here. At last everybody but Pippa had gone. Tom came to see and much impressed went off to the dispensary for a nipple. Zineb watched in doubt and dismay, her dinner preparations at a standstill, while they boiled nipple, bottle, and milk in separate pans. When they finally nudged the nipple into Boot's mouth he tried to take hold but couldn't suck hard enough to bring the milk out. Tom made bigger holes with an ice pick and then Boots gagged and dribbled. Then Pippa and Cathy took turns with an old medicine dropper, holding his mouth open carefully while the milk ran gently down his throat. By then he seemed resigned, exhausted by the struggle, and enchanted them by falling asleep.

"Look at his eyelashes," Cathy whispered.

They loved his cloven hooves. Pippa said, "If he had a horn in his forehead he'd look exactly like a tiny unicorn." Then she wailed, "Cathy, I can't bear to go away now!" Later on she said, "You'll write me everything he does, won't you?" Because he woke and did one marvelous thing after another, like yawning, like blinking, like wrinkling his funny nose and making that shivering bleat. There is something touching about anything new and small, they agreed. Kittens pouncing and snuggling. Puppies trotting and curious. Chicks fluffy and pin-eyed, peeping. Colts were best of all, perhaps, nudging their noses into your hands for sugar and then bolting away with their heads in the air. Even baby caterpillars and baby insects were charming; they might do something interesting any second, like hump themselves in the middle or spin a sudden thread.

Suddenly Boots reared up and vomited into Cathy's lap.

At her cry, Latifa came running. She stood wringing her hands. Mom followed and Latifa said, "Surely he will die."

"We must call Dr. Prescot, he'll know what to do," Pippa said and ran to the telephone.

"It's only that he can't yet handle cow's milk," the doctor said, not in the least surprised. "He is too young. Call Mohammed to the phone and I'll tell him where he can get sheep's milk." Mohammed stood nodding. Then, taking a bottle from the kitchen, he drove away. When he came back it was all to do over again. At first Boots refused to try. But after a time he began once more to swallow.

Pippa's mother telephoned and when Mom told her the trouble she agreed Pippa might stay. "Dinner's ready," Mom said over their bowed heads.

"We're not hungry. We had all that cake."

"Neither of you ate three bites of cake."

Dad laughed and said, "They can have sandwiches later. Maybe this is just what Cathy needed." He was certain of this when the girls decided there was no need to buy a new basket. Foxy's old one was taken from the closet and made into a cozy bed on the terrace.

Boots slept. "In a day or so we can give him a bath."

"I have a ribbon I'll bring over tomorrow."

"I'll always keep him white as snow—"

"Like Mary's lamb! Do you suppose he'll follow you to school? Oh, I *can't go,* Cathy. You'll write everything he does, won't you?"

Later Cathy lay in bed, listening for Boots to stir, but contented. He would never dig under a fence and run away, she thought. He would grow more and more beautiful, like the lambs she had seen on the hills, his wool thicker. When the muezzin spoke from the tower of the mosque, she thought, He is a Moroccan lamb. In this windy, wooly land herds grazed on every other hillside; she had seen small flocks grazing on vacant lots in the middle of the town. That first day she had seen a sheep trotting at the heels of a woman on the road. Now she remembered this with pleasure. Boots would walk with her; she would begin right away to train him.

How right it was to have such a pet in Morocco. She thought of the woolen robes people wore on the streets, of the round woolen caps, brightly colored, that she had seen men knitting in the souks, of the hoods lifted over everybody's heads when it rained. In America, Navajos wore wool, kept warm with blankets of wool from their herds, woven on their own looms. She understood why this was now. In Morocco it was the same: not only because of the wind blowing every day but because there was no other fabric that would keep out wind and rain and even, as she had read, keep out the heat of the sun. The shepherds and all the people must love sheep and the wool that grew abundantly on their backs, under their chins, around their ears, on their long burry tails. She thought almost with awe of how it would be with Boots, who would grow his own thick soft coat during the winter. And in the spring she would shear it off before hot weather came. Once she had seen an Indian woman spinning with a long stick set on a tiny pottery plate with a hole in it. A long thread whirled out of a mass of wool. Now she remembered exactly how it looked. She could get a spindle. Sometime she would have enough wool from Boots to make herself a coat to keep forever. Then one for Pippa. Tomorrow she would tell Pippa about it.

During the night Boots was restless, and she went to the kitchen and warmed more milk. She lay on her bed to feed him. Seeing the light on, Mom came down the hall. "Cathy, for heaven's sake, not on your bed—"

"He's as clean as clean. Anyway, I'm the one to clean up after him." That had always been the rule about every pet.

Mom closed the door and went away. Sometimes, she thought, Cathy's face had a look that was downright beautiful. She wasn't pretty, not like those curly-haired, pink-cheeked French twins. But when there was something small or weak, any animal to take care of, she got this marvelous look.

When Latifa came the next morning she was surprised to find the lamb still alive. She said, "Madame, perhaps another liter of the milk today."

"So much for such a small lamb?" Mom asked.

"*Oui—si*—yes, Madame." Often Latifa said things in all the languages people talked in Tangier. "Ee-yeh," she said it then in Moroccan, "Perhaps three we need. Will be spillings. Until soon this Boots eats himself the grass."

The phone rang. Pippa. She said excitedly, "We

should take Boots to Dr. Prescot right away, for a check-up."

"I was thinking that, too. Maybe there are things like rabies shots for lambs."

"I looked in a book Dr. Prescot has, all about sheep. They can get ticks. And worms."

"Once Foxy had worms . . ." Now she could say his name again without choking. When she hung up Mom looked at her suspiciously. "What was that about worms?" she asked.

"We're taking Boots to the doctor to be sure he hasn't any. And we've got to get him weighed so I can start a record to send Pippa."

The phone rang again.

"I'll answer. It's Pippa again. She had to 'ring off' and said she'd give me 'another tinkle' in a minute." Cathy giggled and Mom smiled too. Here was another English word whose meaning was quite different than in the States where to "tinkle" was common babytalk for going to the toilet. Yes, Pippa, saying, "I've had this *super* idea. This summer when the PDSA has its big bazaar to get money, you and I could have a wool shop. We could have Boots in the shop with us, looking wooly."

"With a nice collar. We can wind it with different colors of yarn."

"Super. It was your idea about spinning and everything that made me think of it. And Cathy, before I go you should start being a member. The PDSA is one of the nicest things in Tangier. Did you know that we have two Royal Highness Princesses for patrons? Princess

Alexandra in England and Princess Lalla Fatima Zahara here in Morocco. She's the King's sister—and she came to our bazaar last summer."

"Good," Cathy said, having to smile at all this Englishness of Pippa. "Maybe we can introduce Boots to Her Royal Highness."

"We've got a real Marquis too and some Honourables and a Lord and some Ladies."

This time Cathy had to say something, feeling suddenly quite American; an odd feeling, half jealous and yet rather smug. "Americans don't have old-fashioned things like lords and ladies. We get to be important because we *do things*," she said.

Pippa sounded a bit sharp. "So do we. Lots of clever people like writers and actors and artists get to be Sirs and Dames, didn't you know that? The Queen decorated the Beatles, remember?" She sounded so dead serious that Cathy decided she'd better say something ridiculous and make her laugh or they might even have a fight.

"Do you think if Boots gets to be really special he might be decorated?"

"Cathy, what an absolutely *weird* thing to say!"

"Anyway, what time shall we go and see about his ticks and worms?"

Then they began to laugh. Cathy sat on the floor, and when they could talk, Pippa said, "I've made a list of things we've got to do before I go. Mum says you can sleep here if your parents agree, and Boots can come too. After the clinic I want to show you the Kasbah; on the way we'll see the Phoenician graves. When they were found they were full of treasures. In the old days people were buried with their jewels and clothes and everything."

"Like the cave dwellers in America. They were Indians. Even their horses and dogs were buried with *them*. I really like that idea, don't you?"

"Let's make wills asking to be buried with our horses and dogs."

"Who'll get Boots in her grave? We'll have to flip a coin, you heads, me tails." This put them into stitches again, and Cathy lay on the floor with the phone on her stomach which had begun to ache with laughing. "We could ask to be buried together. Won't our parents be amazed?"

"But we'll be partner-veterinarians by then. It will seem quite natural."

"And anthropologists too. Why don't we be anthropologists and maybe archeologists, too, so we can dig up old cities and bones and put them together into pet dinosaurs."

Mom said, "For heaven's sakes, Cathy, will you *please* get off that phone? I'm expecting a call."

On the way to the clinic they took turns carrying Boots. His long bony legs were more awkward and he was heavier than they had thought. "Do you know what I can do—weigh him every morning on our bathroom scale the way we weigh our suitcases. You weigh yourself, see, with your suitcases on the floor on either side. Then you pick them up and weigh again and subtract."

"I heard about a farmer who picked up his little

bull calf every day. And even when the calf weighed hundreds of pounds he could still lift him, because he'd got used to it."

"That can't be true. There had to come a day—"

"But he got bigger so gradually, you see."

"All the same, it must have got harder and harder. When Boots is a huge ram, do you think I can still weigh him in our bathroom?"

Pippa looked stricken. "I don't want him ever to be a huge ram, do you?" She looked down at him. "But I'm sure he wants to be. The way we want to be ladies."

Cathy stared at her. "*I* don't want to be a lady," she said. She had never thought about it particularly before. "I just want to be a veterinarian-anthropologist."

They were laughing when they carried Boots into the courtyard at the clinic. A large white egret was walking about on the stones, looking rather lopsided. When it hurried out of the way they saw that it had only one wing. Mustapha was painting purple medicine on a huge, angry-looking sore on the haunch of a small donkey at the same time its baby was nudging it for milk. "Only three days old," Mustapha said, looking patient. "He has never stopped suckling." Dr. Prescot had found the egret when he was out with the ambulance. "And today here is a stork. He had been in a terrible battle with another male who tried to take his nest and drive him away."

What wonderful patients there were in Morocco. Once, Pippa said, there was a gazelle that had lost a horn in a fight. And another time somebody brought in a jackal pup that had been left alone when his mother was shot. A farmer brought a wild piglet that grew quite affectionate and lived very happily with the horses at the Rest Home until somebody shot it as a wild boar by mistake. "Wild boar is delicious, but nobody who ever knew him could bear to eat a bite."

Hearing their voices, Dr. Prescot came out of his office. Seeing Boots, he said, "More trouble already?"

"No, we only want a checkup and advice."

He took one of the tiny polished hooves in his big hand and said, "How do you do, Mr. Boots?" and Boots delighted them by giving a quivering little *maaaaa*.

"We want to keep track of his weight the way you do with Little Owl," Cathy said. It made her feel sad to see the scale where poor Foxy had been weighed such a short time ago. "Nine pounds!" the doctor said. "He'll probably gain about a pound a week for a while, and in a year he's likely to be a hundred-pounder."

"He seems to want to nibble things. How soon should we bring him grass?"

They were very serious, like young mothers, and he spoke seriously too. "He'll soon find what he needs. Later you might try him on some cabbage and lettuce— maybe a bit of bran or barley." He ran his fingers around Boots' gums and looked into his ears and explored his stomach and his bones. "He'll be almost his full size when he's two. In England a four-month ram will weigh from seventy to ninety pounds, but here about half that."

"The difference is *scientific husbandry*," Pippa said. "I read that in the sheep book."

"Maybe," Cathy said, "we could make him so big

and special he'd be the biggest ram in Morocco. Do they have fairs here?" In her mind Boots flowered with ribbons.

Dr. Prescot laughed. "It might take a generation or so to make *that* much difference. In animals *or* fairs. But I must say he looks like something special."

"It's because we brushed him so well and put Sea Shell Shade nail polish on his hooves." Then Pippa asked, "Do you think that might be dangerous? I remember reading somewhere that nail polish can be poisonous."

"Well," he said without so much as a grin, "nobody ever yet brought a sheep in here that had been poisoned from biting his toenails."

The three of them shouted with laughter. "But it *is* all right, isn't it, to bathe him in my tub?" Cathy asked.

"If you can get around his objections and the objections of your housekeeper," he said, "*I* don't have any." But then he became quite serious, running his fingers through Boot's brushed wool. "Watch for lice and ticks. And flies may blow on him and give him a few maggots. I'll give you something for them. But for now . . ." He set Boots down and smiled to see him teeter off on his bony legs, his polished hooves clicking on the tiles. "He's a perfect specimen."

In the room where Foxy had died Cathy now saw things she had been too disturbed to notice before. An odd bunch of paraphernalia hung on one wall, like a curious modern still life—bits of wood and string and leather and wire draped upon long nails. Bird traps, the doctor said, and slingshots taken from boys who were forever capturing migrating birds who crossed Africa at the Straits every spring and fall. Sometimes he feared that mankind meant to drive all wild creatures from the world.

"I'm a member of the Wilderness Society," Cathy said.

"And I'm a member of the Fauna Preservation Society and World Wildlife," said Pippa.

"And now both of you are honored members of PDSA, Tangier, Morocco," said the doctor.

"You know, everybody gets things wrong," Cathy said, "even somebody as bright as Leonardo da Vinci. I read a story about him, how he went to the market in Milan where he lived and bought cages and cages of wild birds from the boys who trapped them, so he could set them free. They called him 'the crazy painter' because he carried the cages off and opened them in the countryside and let all the birds fly away. And all the time—" She blinked.

"All the time he was encouraging the boys to go and trap some more." Dr. Prescot went with them into the sunny courtyard, empty now except for the crippled egret and two pigeons. "There is an English painter in Tangier who is in some ways brighter than Leonardo," he said. "You know him, of course, Pippa—"

"Oh, yes! Cathy, I'll show you his house in the Kasbah. It's Number O—and *House and Gardens* said it's the only O address in the whole world."

"He's also a great storyteller, and he thinks some of the English people here who keep worrying about sick storks and donkeys are quite funny. He says there was an old Moroccan man bringing his produce to market on his donkey. He rode on the donkey and his grandson walked behind. They passed two Moroccan ladies who said to each other, 'See that wicked old man, making that poor little boy walk while he rides!'

"So the old man got down and told the boy to ride for a while. But they passed two more Moroccan ladies who said, 'See that horrid little boy riding while his poor old grandfather walks behind!'

"So they both got onto the back of the donkey and rode along for awhile. Then they met two English ladies who threw up their hands and said to each other, 'See those dreadful, thoughtless Moroccans, riding that poor little donkey. They are so cruel to animals!'

"And the old man sighed and the boy sighed and they both got down and between them carried the donkey to the market."

One night at Pippa's and then one night at Cathy's, they decided. Boots was as happy in one place as the other. Looking as white and smelling as sweet as a fluff of popcorn, he was everybody's darling.

Pippa's mother had their table set on the back terrace, a breezy place smelling of honeysuckle. It was fun comparing their ways of eating. Pippa kept her fork in her left hand in the English manner and pushed food onto the back of it. Cathy used her fork right side up in her right hand to spear things. They tried each other's ways and Pippa said, "Your way is as hard as chopsticks. Moroccans have a better way, they just eat with their fingers. But only with the right hand, the thumb and the two next fingers." They tried that too and smeared their napkins. A large Moroccan dinner, Pippa explained, was called a diffa and happened in a tent.

"You'll surely get invited to one sometime. Watch out for the whole roast lamb—it's set on the table and everybody tears bits off—it's terribly hot. You dip it into a dish of cumin and that makes it hot inside you too."

"There may be a diffa when you come back. In summer, a tent dinner would be in the summer."

"When I come back . . ." "When you come back . . ." It was a refrain now, and Boots kept baaing plaintively as if he were thinking about it too.

Cathy loved a few pieces of very special painted furniture in Pippa's room, familiar now. There was a high clothes chest painted in bright pure colors and a small chest with the same designs, both made of cedar. "Moorish artists are forbidden to paint living things," Pippa said. "It's something to do with worshipping images, my art teacher said. There's a sort of Koranic law about painting or sculpting living things." One of her posters was a copy of an El Greco from the Prado in Spain. "Someday we'll go on trips together and I'll show you how different the painting is in the Prado and in museums in Fez. Spanish painters fill pictures with people and animals. Warriors on horses and Jesus and his sad, long-faced disciples and lots and lots of fat angels and kings and queens in fabulous clothes. And heroes fighting bulls, and pools and pools of blood . . ."

She brought upstairs a big book of photographs of Morocco, and they sat on the bed, turning the pages together. "See, it's mostly pictures of Fez and Marrakesh. Fez is the most beautiful place you can imagine. This summer we can go on a trip—Mum and Dad have promised—and I'll show you. See the tiles—flowers and triangles and arabesques and circles, but not a living creature. Never even a bird among all these leaves. They aren't *our* sort of artists, are they?"

On top of the chest lay a small thick wooly rug. It was because it reminded her so much of Boots that Cathy noticed it especially now. Pure white, it would have looked like a lambskin except that a row of red threads had been woven through, outlining a tower and a tracery of Arabic letters.

"That's my prayer rug," Pippa said seriously. "I helped make it last summer in a workshop in the Kasbah. The woman who runs it is named Lily but I call her the Wool Woman." She took the rug and put it on the floor and knelt on it. "She said I was never to let it be stepped on and I should never put it on the floor unless I knelt on it." She looked rather self-conscious, kneeling there, as if she wondered whether Cathy was the religious type. "Would you like to say your prayers on it too?" she asked.

Half the time Cathy forgot to say any prayer at all, and she felt rather guilty chanting away with Pippa as if she said one every night. Putting the rug again in its place on the chest, Pippa said, "The Arabic letters say *Allah is God*—the words the muezzin chant from the minarets every day. The Wool Woman says we must respect all religions everywhere or we can pray night and day and never get any peace in the world."

"When you come back—" Cathy began.

"Oh, but you must meet the Wool Woman before I go! Then you can go up there whenever you like and see the beautiful things she makes. Dad says she's his idea of a real woman of the world. She's Hungarian, but had to leave her home in Budapest when she was quite young. First she was in Paris and then in London and then came here for a holiday. She says she fell in love with Morocco the first day. And she can say it in seven languages!"

Cathy ran her hand over the little rug. "It feels *real*," she said.

"It *is* real. Lily says she can't bear any of the new artificial fabrics. Everything she does is *pure wool*." They sat cross-legged on the floor, like Buddhas in their nightgowns. "She felt just the way we do about the grass and trees and flowers and the sheep grazing and the shepherds in their robes. Then she saw Moroccan women spinning as they watched their children and animals in the fields. So she 'tried with her own hands the spinning' and then got herself an old handmade loom. Then another one. Then a Moroccan weaver helped her, and she began to make her own designs and to dye her own colors. Then more looms and more weavers. So now her rugs and fabrics are famous with designers and architects everywhere."

Pippa's mother knocked on the door and said, "Time to pack up, you two."

They lay silent, wide awake. "I couldn't bear the thought of going off to school now," Pippa said, "if I didn't know I was coming back and that we're going to Fez together. Until you and Boots, Fez was my greatest thing in my whole life. There's a shop where they make tiny Hands of Fatima, golden filigree. Maybe we can save up and get two—for each other."

"Then we can always wear them, wherever we go."

They lay quiet and beyond the consulate walls they could hear people talking and laughing on the street. One high clear voice was singing. "That's the blind beggar who always sits outside the gate," Pippa said. "He's singing verses from the Koran, about almsgiving. I give him a franc every day; it's supposed to bring you a blessing if you give alms."

A donkey brayed. Hooves clattered on the rough stones of the street. "Tomorrow's market day," Pippa whispered. "The farmers are coming already. Listen—"

The sound of people was different here, Cathy thought. Even at a distance, the sound, the rhythm of languages is different.

"Don't you simply *love* strange places?" Pippa asked.

Cathy lay silent for a moment. "No," she said. "Not really. Remember I told you that first day."

Pippa did not answer. Their hands met on the covers. Now, lying in the dark, they could say it all.

"See, I was quite little and our first place was England. Liverpool. That's why I expected you to be so awful. I told Mom I knew you'd be stiff and snooty for a long time, longer than you'd *be* here. I went to a girl's school in Liverpool and for a solid year hardly anybody spoke to me at all. First they asked questions about America, sort of crowding around *interviewing*, you know what I mean. I was just a curiosity. Nobody could remember an American in that school before. Then I was left alone—absolutely alone, all day, every day pretending to be lost in books, and all night, every night trying to be really lost in them. Just the last month there were two girls, Jenny and Anne—they began to be friendly and we had fun together. But Jenny thought I was trying to come between them. Anne told me they quarreled about it and that Jenny *hated* me."

Pippa murmured, "I'm sorry it was England that was the worst. I thought the *other places* were—"

"Not the worst. I didn't mean that. I was so little then and so mixed up and lonely and I cried all the time. Tom was disgusted with me, crying so much. Then this doctor-friend of Dad's visited us. He was studying psychology and doing some sort of study about State Department kids. He kept asking me why I kept crying—"

"As if you could tell him *that!*" Pippa's voice sounded pained and angry.

"I tried to. I really did. The thing was, feeling strange all the time, and alone. So he said how lucky I was, having such nice parents and how splendid it was that Mom never turned me over to servants the way some mothers do."

Then it was Pippa's turn, her voice rapid and somehow *hot* as if her breath came steaming. "He was right, you at least went to school where your parents were. You saw them at night, and when you cried they were *there*—"

"I cried by myself."

"But they were in the same *house;* I was in a dormitory. For years I *lived* for holidays. Three times a year our Foreign Service sends us wherever our parents are, even if it's China or Australia."

"I dreaded holidays. Dad needed to rest and they went off places."

"Of course that's sensible—"

"Oh, my parents are *sensible. Too* sensible."

"The big trouble is, by the time you get settled and start feeling at home, you have to start packing up again."

"You get to feeling as if you were just another bit of *baggage.*"

They lay with closed eyes. Then Cathy said, "Pippa? I've got a wonderful idea. When Dad first told us about Tangier, the first thing on the Advantages List was 'Has American School with very high rating. Numbers of graduates win scholarships in America's finest universities.' So . . . " She took a deep breath. "Do you think your folks might be willing to let you go to my school—just this year?"

Pippa did not answer for a time. Then she said, "No, they'd never think of it. They always say, 'It would be very nice to have you at home, Pippa, but you mustn't miss any of the courses or you won't pass your exams.' It's terribly important in England to pass exams. They might even say what my English teacher does at this awful school—English and American are two different languages."

"They really aren't."

"But they sort of are." They both sighed. It was just another thing, this time the most important thing, they had never been able to do anything about.

"But just now we're *here,*" Pippa said.

"Wasn't it lucky we happened to be here at the same time?" Peaceful with this wonder, they lay quiet

"And there's next summer. And Fez. My father promised me we'd go by the mountain road around sun set, the way we did before. I want you to get that fabulous view—I can hardly wait to show you. And we'll go to this shop I told you about and get Hands of Fatima so we'll never forget each other."

"We wouldn't forget, anyway," Cathy said, feeling a pang of fear at the thought.

"Of course not. But they'll be *signs*."

They lay listening to the beggar chanting. And fell asleep. And woke to Sunday with birds singing in the trees and donkeys braying in the market. Pippa ran to the window and called, "It's so clear today we can see Spain and Gibraltar." Fishing boats stood far out.

Pippa was expected to go to church at Easter and Cathy was pleased to go along, feeling very important to be ushered to the front pew by a man with a long, official-looking staff that had a golden crown on the tip. Just as she began to tell Pippa how she enjoyed this, Pippa whispered: "I *loathe* being made important like that, don't you? All the people looking."

It was the prettiest church Cathy had ever seen. The ceiling was like a huge carving, all in bright colors like Pippa's furniture. The altars were decorated with plaster tiles in intricate designs, lacy white, and there were bright red carpets and prayer stools and altar railings. Flowing Arabic words made part of the design around a central arch at the front, and Pippa whispered, "That's the Lord's Prayer in Arabic!"

Cathy wasn't sure, during the service, when she must kneel, sit, stand, so she played Follow the Leader with Pippa. During some of the long prayers she read some of the memorial plaques around the walls. Two told sad stories:

In Memory of
William Barrie Ritchie,
who died at sea on April 1905
on his way back from Ireland to Tangier.

Probably buried in one of those canvas bags, she thought, so this was his only gravestone.

In Memory of Thomas Green
R.A.F. 1937
Bomber Command 1939
Prisoner of War 1941
Shot After Escaping March 25, 1944.

Her skin prickled, thinking about it. In parentheses under the dates were the words "GOOD HUNTING, TIM."

One in front was red-lettered, honoring John Drummond Hay, PC CCMC KGB. A Governor of Tangier. She must ask Pippa what all the important letters meant. Pippa saw her looking and smiled, whispering, "Grandpa told me he married a Danish woman and Hans Christian Andersen came to Tangier to visit them!"

"Really, Pippa? The *real Ugly Duckling?*"

"The real Ugly Duckling. There's a description of Tangier in his diary. There was no harbor then and he was carried ashore 'on the shoulders of strong brown Moors . . .' "

"Sssssh. . . ." Pippa's mother gave them a warning look and they sat still until the last slow hymn and the last long prayer had ended.

"That plaque should say *Hans Christian Andersen was here,*" Cathy said.

At the back of the church was another romantic story carved in stone. *Emily, the Shareefa of Wazan.* "She came to be a schoolteacher just like Anna of Siam," Pippa said, "and married a shareef and lived to be ninety-five years old." From the arched doorway they saw many more English ladies, in hats and gloves, drinking punch together in the sun. "You'd expect them to be boring," Pippa whispered, "but they're not. They're all members of PDSA and have lovely houses and dogs and cats and horses—and the Rector has fourteen storks living on his roof!"

They rushed to feed Boots. They had decided to crush two multiple vitamin pills into his milk every day.

Over the telephone Pippa made her voice into a romantic growl that Cathy knew came from an ancient film about a sheik of Araby: "Today I vill take zee to zee *Kasbah!*" Then, in her own voice, "Really, Cathy, some of the girls at my school never heard anything about Arabs except sheiks in flowing white robes carrying women off on white horses."

"My best friend in Washington thought all Arabs were forever riding in long lines of camels over endless deserts. And Tom's friends only knew Arabs have lots of oil and overcharge us for it."

"And poor Morocco hasn't a pint of oil!"

Pippa planned to go in a circle, up the long way by Avenue Hassan II and straight down the steps of the medina to midtown. The streets on the way had lovely names. One was Mordejay Bengio. Who could *he* have been? There was no use learning the names, Cathy could see, because they didn't go on and on like Regent Street or Wisconsin Avenue. "They change every block or so," Pippa said. "And anyway now the Spanish and French names are being changed to Arabic ones. So just as you think you're one place, you find you're in another. Tangier is full of surprises. You can be invited to tea behind a wall with one door—and find yourself in a huge house with gardens and fountains and birds and servants dressed like Turkish sultans!"

Once she left the streets and they went along a dusty road that led to old graves cut in boulders above the sea. Back again they climbed a steep little hill that ended in an arch and high stone walls. Sudden alleys went off to the right and there were dozens of doors, all colors, carved, brass-studded doors, all different with heavy old locks. Then another arch opened, long and cool and windy. It framed the harbor far below, alive with yachts and ferries and one long white ship.

"And here we are!" Pippa turned into a cobbled passage which had a high lacy iron door at the back. *Raid Sultan 9. Moroccan Arts and Crafts. Tapis. Carpets.*

Double doors were marked *No entrée,* and Pippa knocked three times, slowly and firmly. "That's our special sign, Lily's and mine," she said. And the door opened. There, in a huge orange caftan lively with black embroidery, stood the Wool Woman.

"*Entrez!* Welcome to the house!" She said it, "well *come,*" as if that gave it a better meaning of her own, and kissed Pippa on both cheeks the way French people do every time they meet. "And this must be Cath—*ee!*" Cathy got her French kisses too. "Pippa has told me all about," she said.

Pippa was right, there was no way to describe the Wool Woman's talk. She mixed up languages and pronunciations in the most marvelous ways imaginable, and Cathy liked her at once.

"They are needing wool—*un momento,* I am in the wool room," she said, and put on a little mask to protect her nose and mouth from dust. The outline of her lips was printed on it in lipstick, from wearing it before, which gave her a pleasantly absurd look, especially dressed in her voluminous caftan. "Pippa, you will show Cath-ee; I join you at the roof for a mint tea. *Si Absalom!*" and she began ordering the tea.

They wandered through a huge room, lively with upright looms on which thick carpets were being made, brown, white, bordered and triangled in different colors. Rows of black-haired girls and women, all ages from seven to fifty, were tying knots, working with such rapid fingers Cathy could not see how the knots were made. *Snip-snip* went scissors, *thump-thum*p went iron forks that tamped the knots as tightly together as the wool on Boots's back. Three flat looms were busy making fabrics on a balcony at one side, going *bang-bang* every time the shuttles went striking through. A man sat on his haunches whirling thread onto a wheel made of bamboo. Others filled shuttles with scarlet and green.

"Look, this wool room is my favorite," Pippa

said and drew Cathy into an immense closet hung with swatches of wool in every color you could dream of, each in graduated shades from light to dark. Some was very fine for the fabrics, some heavy and thick for the carpets. From the looms they heard the girls singing a wailing kind of song which must be a Moroccan ballad in time with the thumping of the looms. The thumping was rhythmic, like drumming, and one high voice sang a verse alone—that would tell the story, Cathy knew—and then all the voices sang a refrain together, over and over, as they started up a steep winding stairs.

The singing stopped suddenly and they heard Lily's voice from the big room, giving advice to the weavers, and apparently giving them a scolding while she was about it. "She says they forget the design the minute her back is turned," Pippa said, "and rows and rows have to be taken out and done all over."

Stepping into brilliant sunshine was staggering. Other rooftops were piled up helter-skelter as far as one could see, chimneys and towers and balconies and turrets and a mosque with a tower set on top of a bigger tower, waving a small green flag. A room had been built on this roof, at the back, for washing and dyeing, and long skeins of wool, brown and white and red and yellow, dried on lines in the sun. Toward the new town they could see a clutter of streets and apartment buildings and the long curve of city beaches lined with restaurants. The white liner was now moving lazily out to sea. Voices and footsteps could be heard from the narrow streets below. Suddenly a sheep made a plaintive baa-aaaa from one of the rooftops.

A sheep up here? When Lily came panting from the stairway, she said, "The poor sheeps—we try not to think of this at the moment. Every house a holy ram fattening for the feast of Aid El Kabir." She waved an arm over the town, shining white in the sun. "But now we enjoy only the vision of beauty in this place." Her orange robe fluttered in the breeze and her dark hair blew back from her face. "I have joy looking at the same scene for now thirty years!"

A few steps led down to another part of the roof and there a circle of girls sat working. Lily called to them in Arabic, and then said to Cathy and Pippa in English without pausing for a breath between languages, "You see, after much washing and dyeing and working, still there remain burrs and grasses and seeds the sheeps have gathered in the wool. *Naturelle*—you understand? In the crafts—works of the hand—nature of animal, hands of worker, all remain."

An Arab boy appeared with a tray holding three steaming glasses of tea. A small round wooden table was set before three cushions against a wall. It was luxurious to sit in the sun, their legs stretched out, and sip sweet tea from glasses filled with crushed green leaves. "The mint is good for what ails," Lily said. "Here is always drunk at the finish of a great feast, for the digestion." She showed Cathy how to hold the hot glass comfortably, by the bottom and top, with spread fingers.

As they talked and drank, the mournful baaing of the sheep came again over the rooftops. Cathy did not mention it again, but Lily looked at her and said, "Pippa has told me of the small lamb, Boots, who is black only on the ears and nose and legs. A true Moor, this one. Everywhere I have traveled the sheeps are alike—there is a saying 'as alike as two sheeps,' yes? But in Morocco is not so. In the fields and in the market is found every shade of white and gray and brown and black."

"When Boots grows some wool," Cathy said shyly, "I thought I could shear it and weave it into a prayer rug like the one you gave Pippa."

"Good! But a long time for one small sheep to grow so much. A big sheep gives perhaps two kilo in one season and for a *tapi*, a rug—even a small one . . ." Lily spread her hands. "Your rug must be the gift of many animals. We will go to the wool market together—there each woman is selling wool from her own. We will arrange."

When they stood up to go and looked down at the view once more, she said, "Every sheep, like the small Boots, is different. If you notice in the streets, the people too, each different. Dressed in his own way, each for his own life. It is because of these things I fell in love with Morocco. I came as a tourist, like the crowd walking every day in the Kasbah."

One of the workers came from the dyeing room to ask Lily a question about two bits of wool in his hand. She spoke to him rapidly, no, no, it was not right, why did he not see it? Then she said, "You see—here is no peace. My back is turned one moment and the work is spoiled."

She called after them, "Big kiss! Big kiss!" as they went down the stairs and once more into the long shady arch through which a cool wind was blowing. A crowd of tourists, obviously American, were being guided through. "Stand to the wall," a guide called out as an old man appeared driving a donkey loaded with huge baskets of charcoal. Cathy got a rich donkey-whiff as he brushed past and gave him a pat. He turned his head and showed his long teeth at her as if he were grinning.

The tourists, hung with cameras, were delighted. "I got that donkey grinning at that girl!" a woman squealed. Walking on ahead, Cathy thought how odd it was, the minute she went abroad she began feeling responsible for Americans and everything America itself did in the world. It couldn't be only because she was a State Department Brat. Tom was one too, but the minute *he* was abroad he began to pretend he was a native who knew all about the place and was superior to mere tourists passing through.

They came out again into a blaze of sun on the huge Kasbah square. As the tourists arrived a dark man in a striped turban and long full Turkish pants began to charm a snake out of a basket. A tambourine and a drum and a reed flute made weird music to which the hooded cobra writhed as he lifted himself, coil after coil, his tongue flicking.

Cameras again. The dark man hung the snake around his neck while pictures were taken, and then held it out. Who would like to have his picture taken with a cobra about his neck? One man laughed and stepped forward. "They won't believe this back in Dubuque!" he said.

A woman rushed forward. "I heard about a man

who did that in the square in Marrakesh—and an hour later he died!"

Cathy and Pippa felt sorry for the snake, which had had an operation, they knew, to remove all of its venom. They went across the square and into the museum where they walked slowly around, staring at ancient things. Then outside again, they walked down narrow flights of steps that sometimes twisted, suddenly revealing tiled fountains or brass-studded doors.

"Look, there's a Hand of Fatima knocker," Pippa said. It was the likeness of a woman's hand with a ring on one finger. "She was the daughter of Mohammed and her hand is supposed to protect the house. The hands for our necklaces will be the same—but tiny and delicate." Pippa smiled. "They will protect us all the same."

In the middle of the houses and narrow shops called souks they heard a curious sound. Children were chanting together. Their voices were high and clear and the rhythm of their chant sounded like that of the voices the girls heard in the night. "A Koranic school," Pippa said. "They are learning to read." They could see through the open door a roomful of small boys sitting on the floor. Each held a slate and a pencil. A man with a long stick stood in front. He paid no attention to Pippa and Cathy, but several of the boys did and began to stare and whisper. Suddenly the stick came out to remind them to pay attention.

"Oh, dear," Pippa said, and they hurried off, straight into the swarm of the market.

"Pippa—*smell!*" Cathy breathed deep, spices and lemons and oranges and mint, incense and flowers and woodsmoke. "Everything seems magic today," she said.

Then they almost collapsed with laughter because a wind suddenly brought them the terrible stink of the fish market.

Boots gained another pound before Pippa's last day. He followed them briskly as they walked around the garden, now and then performing a small gallop.

"He's so clever," Pippa said. "It takes pups much longer to learn to heel."

"Tom says he's not really heeling, he's just doing what lambs always do, following whoever provides the food."

"We haven't any food right *now*," said Pippa.

"Tom thinks he knows everything about everything," Cathy said. "I hope he doesn't talk the whole time at lunch the way he usually does. When he goes on and on and *on* I call him Tom-Tom." And she added, "That's an Indian drum. An *American* Indian drum."

"Of course," Pippa said.

The table was set on the terrace under a huge striped parasol and looked very nice. But Cathy's heart sank because Tom said at once, acting cocky, "You'd better stop fattening that precious lamb of yours. If he gets too big and juicy somebody will eat him."

It pleased Cathy to see Pippa giving him her cool British shoulder. "Only huge, grown rams are killed for the feast," she said. "Last year I went with my parents to see the sheep market in Asilah and there were *no* small lambs at all."

He chanted: "From little acorns great oaks grow,
From little lambs great rams!"

Mom said, "Please, Tom, don't be ugly."

"I'm not being ugly, I'm just giving them the facts of life. Cathy thinks all the nice sheep following people around the streets lately are lovey-dovey pets like her Bootsie-Wootsie. But they're all being fattened up for the knife."

"I must say I don't think it's necessary to talk about that just now, Tom," Dad said.

"Why not? Tomorrow's Aid el Kabir, and I've been reading up on it. Every Moroccan family has to have a sheep for the big feast, just like every family back home has to have a turkey for Thanksgiving."

Pippa said, "And in England, a goose for Christmas."

Zineb had prepared a beautiful couscous for lunch and Latifa set it in the center of the table now. A high pile of saffron-colored semolina was surrounded with vegetables, and in the center lay a nest of tender chicken and lamb. Shiny, thinly sliced onions cooked with raisins lay over the top and toasted almonds were sprinkled around the whole. Everyone had been provided with a big serving spoon.

"How splendid," Dad said deliberately sounding British.

Tom grinned, serving himself, and said, "Well here's to somebody's pet."

"Really, Tom," Mom said, "you're not being in the least funny. And don't eat with your fingers."

"Why not? I figure, when in Rome . . ."

Dad said nothing and Mom gave him a cross look. "Ward, you might tell your son that whether we're in Morocco or not, he will eat properly at his mother's table. We've discussed this before, if I remember."

Cathy hoped they wouldn't argue in front of Pippa. She carefully avoided the lamb and took something of everything else, as Pippa did.

"See, you're a couple of soft Westerners," Tom said. "Everything nicey-nicey, right? All our meat wrapped in cellophane without a drop of blood in sight."

"Tom—" Mom began.

But he said, speaking to Pippa, "Are people the same in England as in America? I've known kids who don't even know milk and meat *come* from animals."

Dad spoke before Pippa could answer. "It is a lot more civilized, isn't it, Tom, to attend to such things in slaughterhouses? I must say I don't relish seeing sheep killed in the streets. Do you?"

"Sure I do. This is the most important Moroccan feast with a thousand years or so of tradition behind it. I'm planning to go out in the morning and watch. Abdulatif told me about a good place—"

"Nobody kills animals in the street!" Cathy's voice was horrified.

Even Tom sat silent for a second. Looking around at Mom, at Dad, even at Pippa, Cathy remembered the way people had been avoiding that subject. Pippa touched her hand under the table. "Only for Aid el Kabir," she said. "Last year we went off to Gibraltar for the day of the feast—a lot of people do. Some of my father's staff left yesterday for Spain."

Tom could be cool too. Now he spoke to Pippa rather respectfully and thoughtfully. "Everywhere we go, see, I make a point of reading up on history and things. About what different people do and their celebrations and all that. Aid el Kabir means "The Big Day" —who'd want to skip out on The Big Day? It's in the month of Chul Hijja, the twelfth month of the Hegiran year."

"Well, now we *know,* don't we, Pippa?" Dad said in his teasing voice. But Cathy knew he really enjoyed the way Tom got busy and learned interesting things about every country they went to. He might tease Tom about being "Big Authority on Everything," even moon ships and math puzzles, but he was always proud of it just the same.

"Do you know what the Hegiran year is, Dad?" Tom asked.

"Of course. It's the calendar Mohammedans follow."

"Do you know how it's different from ours?"

"Well—I think I do. Let's see—" There was a long and rather embarrassed pause.

"It's *lunar,* see? Eleven days shorter than the Christian year. There are some tables I got to figure it out on. It starts from our year 622. Mohammed's relations were persecuting him and he had to get out of Mecca. So he went on this hegira—that's Arabic for a *trip,* see, a sort of pilgrimage—over to Medina—"

Dad laughed. "And ever since that day, boys have been persecuting their relations."

They all laughed and Latifa came to take away the remains of the couscous and to bring a French strawberry tart. She set it down with a big bowl of whipped cream at Mom's place. Dishing it up, Mom said, "I'm glad these rich tarts don't have double crusts like American pies. All this rich food and all the parties. We've never been in a place that had so many parties. Your mother and I, Pippa, agree that pretty soon we won't be able to get into anything but caftans."

"That's all right with me," Dad said. "One Moroccan thing I really do enjoy is the loose, flowing clothes. And sandals without heels. I wish all diplomats and their families were required to wear the clothes of the country."

"So do I," Pippa said. "I wear my caftans in the evening at school and everybody loves them."

Cathy felt her heart sink. She was not going to think about Pippa and the evenings at her school. Just then, as if he thought it high time their lunch was over, Boots began making plaintive *baaas* from the terrace. Pippa and Cathy looked at each other. Tom grinned but didn't bring up the subject of fat lambs again. Pippa made a pretty speech to Mom, thanking her for the good lunch, and Cathy knew she would hear again, after Pippa left, about the beautiful manners of English children.

Latifa had already warmed the milk. While they were taking turns with the bottle, Tom came out onto the terrace and stood watching. "All I meant to say . . ." He spoke rather gently for Tom. "See, the kids of diplomats should be especially interested in what people are like in our host countries. Especially their holy days." He pronounced it holy days and not holidays.

71

Pippa said, "I couldn't agree more."

"Well, on this particular holy day, there'll be a little blood on the streets. But that doesn't make me stop wanting to see the celebration."

Pippa did not answer for a moment, but concentrated on Boots and how he lay, almost like a kitten, sucking away with milk running down from his funny mouth onto a napkin. Then she said, "I suppose my parents thought it wasn't really the sort of thing for me to see."

"Why not?"

"I never asked," Pippa said.

"Because you're a girl?" he asked.

She looked up at him and it seemed to Cathy that her look was almost like flirting. "No—it's nothing to do with being a girl. It's just . . . maybe *taste,*" Pippa said.

They were silent while Dad and Mom strolled across the terrace toward the garden and Dad's office.

"Our American Thanksgiving is sort of like Aid el Kabir," Tom said. "We *call* it Thanksgiving, anyway. But last year I had to remind Dad to ask a blessing at our big turkey dinner."

Mom had come back. Hearing, she said rather crossly, "Thanksgiving isn't exactly a religious day, is it? Not a Church Feast Day, like Christmas and Easter."

"It's supposed to be our Thanking God day, isn't it?" Tom demanded. "The official United States of America Thanking God Day?"

"But that's historical, Tom, not religious."

"It was religious to the Puritans. And they

killed their own meat, too. I can show you a picture of a lot of Pilgrims with a bunch of dead turkeys and bloody axes."

Cathy said, "That's not one of the pictures I've seen. They were always walking to church in a row or sitting by a table with Indians bringing corn and turkeys and pumpkins."

"And now everybody goes to the supermarket and get bloodless turkeys frozen in plastic."

Cathy thought of the live chickens she saw in the Tangier market, their legs tied together and their heads twisting, their bead-eyes looking terrified.

Latifa appeared to call Mom to the telephone.

"If you think you're going to make us want to go—" Cathy began.

But Tom said, "I couldn't care less whether you go or not. I just wanted to make a point, that's all." And then, as if he read her mind, "You can *be* chicken, it's okay by me."

Pippa asked, suddenly looking up, "How early?"

"Around ten, Abdulatif says."

Cathy started to say something but Pippa gave her a warning look and said briskly, "Perhaps we should go and see it, Cathy. As he says, it's *real*. And if we're really going to be vets. . . ."

That afternoon they had a wonderful farewell ride. This time they went into the pet cemetery, tying the horses at the gate while they moved pensively among low white stones. No Foxys, but a dozen other favorite pet names. *For Our Faithful Friend Beau. For Our Be-*

loved Fifi. Towser. Brownie. So many. Then they rode once more to the Rest Home with sugar for the old animals grazing in the field.

"Whenever I come here I think of that old book, *Black Beauty,*" Pippa said. "It's frightfully sloppy, a silly old book, I guess. But I always cry when I read it."

"I still read it too," Cathy said. "I love animal books." How could they not, their eyes asked each other. "Even if some people, like Tom-Tom for instance, says they're corny, I *never* thought so."

"One thing we could do—make lists of our favorite books, and then we can talk about them. We could trade the ones both of us don't know. We could *send* them—"

When an old horse and a tired ragged mule came walking slowly to the fence for sugar, Pippa asked, "Do you suppose I'll ever see Brandy and Soda again? They'll probably *die* before I get back."

Leaning together on the fence, they found it difficult to speak. Everything had the feeling of tomorrow's separation. Even the enchanting smells, when they rode again, that a small rain had brought out of the pines and eucalyptus.

Dad and Mom were not at dinner, having gone with Pippa's parents to an official celebration for some visiting dignitary. Even Tom seemed subdued for a change, sensing their mood. Over dessert he said, "I looked up the story of the sacrifice today—in the Koran. The muezzin will be singing those verses tomorrow morning, I guess. Would you like to hear them?" He had the book all ready, they saw, the place marked with a golden thread.

Cathy looked at Pippa, hoping she would say she had decided not to go with him in the morning, after all.

Pippa said, "I've heard it, but I'd like to hear it again. The Rector read it at St. Andrews last year—and the Bible story of Abraham as well." She was not going to let Tom be either more clever or more brave than she was, Cathy could see.

Tom looked quite handsome with his head bent over the book. "It begins about Abraham and his 'sweet-natured son,'" he said. "'When he had reached an age to help his father, Abraham said: O my son! I have seen in a dream that I was sacrificing thee! . . . He answered, O my father! Do what thou art bidden! Abraham laid the child down upon his forehead and God called to him, O Abraham, you believed in your dream! . . . I ordain in place of your son a sacrifice.'"

Pippa said, "The Bible story is much more exciting. The Koran leaves out all the exciting bits. About Abraham piling the wood up and tying Isaac on top. Isaac didn't even *know* what was going to happen. He asked, 'Where is the lamb for the sacrifice?'"

Tom looked very respectful. "That's right," he said. "And they found the ram caught by its horns in a thicket, all ready for the knife."

Cathy felt left out. She stood up and said, "Well, *our* lamb is ready for his supper. And his bath."

Tom called after them, "See you in the morning!"

Boots's bath had come to seem a precious ritual. Now they both felt but did not need to say that it might be the last time they would accomplish it together. They put some blue in the water to make his wool even whiter. He hated water the way Foxy had and looked just as comically long and skinny with his wool wet. They fluffed him with the hair dryer and when he was brushed he was so beautiful they tied a huge silly blue ribbon on his neck to complete the picture of a character in a nursery book. They took a flash picture of him lying on the bed.

"Take lots and lots of pictures for me, won't you, Cathy? Nobody at school will *believe* him."

When they woke again it would be the day when Pippa would go away.

Pippa turned over and found her hand. "Cathy, I'm sorry how it's working out—the very day—but all of a sudden I just felt I had to *show* him. If a boy could take it, we could. Do you see what I mean?"

Cathy sighed. For a minute she was silent, and they could hear the sounds of celebration music in the town below, around the mosque. Drums and flutes and clapping and a refrain repeated over and over by shrill female voices. Like the girls in the Kasbah. Finally she said, "You don't have a brother, or you'd know how it is. I decided ages ago that I'd never again try to prove to Tom how brave I was, about bull fights and things like that. He doesn't pretend to be nice to me, why should I try to be brave for him? I'd much rather be nice than brave."

"Yes—I see. I really do. But unless you're brave you're really in trouble. Like when you have to go away."

Now Cathy thought a new thing. "Or stay, when somebody else is going," she said. "Before, I've always been the one to go."

"Riding will help, won't it? You here and me there. When I first went off to school I was frightened of horses—imagine! But then I found this particular horse—Charliehorse they called him, a lovely bay—and I could go out and ride on those hedgy English roads. When you come to England I'll show you how perfect it is for riding."

"When you come to Washington you'll love the towpath along the river—"

"There was a French girl at school who was Foreign Service too, and we got to know each other when we couldn't say anything except horse-talk to each other."

"Is she still there?" Cathy felt a stab of jealousy.

"Of course not. I *said* she was Foreign Service, too." And then Pippa said a really important thing: "Do you see how lucky we are to speak the same language, Cathy, even though we're from different countries? Even though my teacher says English and American are not the same, they really are, you know. All the words that are really real and important are the same. That French girl—everything she said had an odd accent and she talked like a tourist. She couldn't say anything *important*—just 'hello' and 'good-bye' and 'thank you' and 'where is the loo'."

Cathy had to laugh. "Remember when I asked you what the loo *was?*"

"Yes. And I tried to explain that typical example of English humor, which is rather different too." Cathy remembered. "Everybody knows that a WC is a water closet, really a nice way to say toilet. Then somebody thought about *Waterloo.*"

They had agreed that the jokes from country to

country were the hardest things of all to understand. It was easy to learn that Pippa's *lift* was Cathy's *elevator,* her *jumper* Cathy's *sweater,* her *tube* Cathy's *subway,* her *torch* Cathy's *flashlight.* The really important words were all the same. *Horse* and *dog* and *flower* and *tree, brother* and *sister* and *parents* (though Pippa's *Mum* was Cathy's *Mom*) , *hate* and *love* and *friend.* And *lamb!* they said together. They made a list. And they agreed that it was terribly important that they both said, "The sky is *blue." Azul* might say the proper color for a Spaniard, the short *bleu* for a Frenchperson, not to speak of *zarac* for an Arab. *Their* sky and sea were forever bluuuuuuuuuuuue!

They said "Good night," glad that *good* and *night* were exactly the same for them and trying not to think about tomorrow's "good-bye."

Tom said, excited, "Did you hear all the guns?" And as they started off he added, "That means the Governor has stabbed the first ram and it's been carried to the mosque. Abdulatif told me that if it's alive when it gets there everybody believes they'll have a lucky year."

Cathy wished Pippa would not feel she had to keep up with Tom, but she said nothing, only hurried even when she began to pant and got a pain in her side. The streets felt oddly alive though few people walked along them this morning. When they turned off the Boulevard de Paris they saw a group of people around a blazing fire. From a distance it looked romantic and pleasant, like a picnic fire. But then Cathy saw the horror and stopped stark still, appalled. A stream of blood was running down the cobblestones into the gutter. A big ram, his horns lifted, his legs twitching, was stretched out on the dirty stones. Blood was gushing from a huge wound in his throat. She saw his eyes. They moved. She cried, "Oh, Pippa—he's still alive!"

A boy came from the crowd by the fire, grinning. He seemed to know Tom. He ran the edge of his hand along his throat, laughing and looking back at the ram, making a click of his tongue. Like cutting.

Cathy did not care about bravery—or even about Pippa, now. She simply turned and ran. She did not notice her own panting or her heart thumping or the pain in her side. Until she got to her own gate she didn't once look back. She was alone. She began to cry and the guard saw her and swung the gate open without a word.

In her room she lay with the sheet pulled over her face, trying to shut the scene out. She thought, every family—all over the country, and in all the other Arab countries as well, thousands and thousands of sheep lay bleeding. She pressed her fingers over her eyes.

Pippa and Tom were quiet at lunch. They ate on the balcony and nobody mentioned the smoke drifting over the town or the smell of burning. When Tom went out to see the people working on the rooftops, preparing their family feasts, Pippa did not go along. There were only a few hours left.

"I'm sorry I didn't come with you this morning, when you ran," she said. "But—well, when I see films with a lot of blood and mess in them, I don't shut my eyes any more. I used to. Now I just set my teeth and look at everything."

Cathy said, "I don't. And if I see it's going to be that kind of film, I just don't *go*. And if it's on TV, I *don't watch*."

"But Tom said something quite wonderful on the way home, Cathy. The Moroccans think it's a fine thing for a beautiful animal to die for The Great Feast. It's a sort of holy death. Like the death of a brave soldier in the old times. Can't you see what they mean? Riding a white horse straight into the spears of the enemy."

"I don't go to war pictures either," Cathy said. "If it was *your* horse—if it was Tarik—would you ride him straight into the spears?"

Pippa had no chance to answer. The car had arrived to take her home. "I've got to go and finish packing. But you're going to the airport with us, aren't you? Do you think we might take Boots?"

Her father said no, for heaven's sakes, the big black British car was full enough with all of Pippa's luggage and her mother's too, since she was going along to see Pippa safely into school. The girls must sit up front with the chauffeur as it was. On the way to the airport they saw the plane, circling down over the sea.

Pippa said, agonized, "Mum, when I come back in July we can go on that trip, can't we? The trip you've talked about. And Cathy can go with us—?"

Just as Mom always said it, Mum answered, "We'll see—"

"But you've always *said*—"

They reached the airport and in the jostling crowds arriving and departing they could think of nothing to say. But right at the last, with the barrier between them, Pippa said, "The first time I was alone at school, I wrote a sort of *diary letter* to Mum and Daddy, a little each day, and mailed it once a week. We could do that!"

She was swept away in the line. "Yes," Cathy called after her. "I'll start *today!*" But a huge voice cut her off, announcing Pippa's plane.

The car seemed big and empty with only Cathy and Pippa's father in the wide back seat. He did not try to make talk, only patted her hand when she got out at home. A kind and understanding man. He saw she was—and wanted to be—entirely alone.

Among her things she had a special box of stationery she liked so much she could never bear to send one sheet away. It had a picture of a different horse on every sheet. Now she knew that she had been saving it for Pippa all along.

What was today? She only knew that it was AP1, one day after Pippa. What could she write so soon? Nothing had happened except. . . . What a wonderful idea! She wrote:

> Cathy took me for a walk down the hill and we saw a herd of sheep. They were *filthy*. Their tails were rusty-red, the color of the ground, and sticky with burrs. I felt very superior and civilized to be clean and white with my blue ribbon. Cathy tried to make me walk with my head up, pulling on my leash. She doesn't seem to know that sometimes, among the stones, I find a blade of grass.
>
> Love,
BOOTS

The next day a really Pippa-thing happened.

Cathy and I walked to the post office down by the American Information Center. She wanted to go in and get some pretty stamps to put on your letters. I had to wait outside. The man who guarded the cars on that street said he would guard me, too. Lots of people stopped to look at me and laughed. They had never before seen a parked lamb. Cathy gave him ten francs.

We won't wait a whole week to mail this first diary-letter because it seems like a week already.

Big kiss,
BOOTS

Cathy thought, today Pippa is in school in England and I am alone in Africa. But she was glad school was starting, glad to hear American all around her when she and Mom went to see the Headmaster. It was a pretty school with a chimney like a ship's smokestack and lots of balconies. As they entered the circling drive between lawns and flowers, the car gave a terrific bump, and Mom said, "Good. That is to stop the speeders. Somebody here is thinking." And when the Headmaster began to speak she said, "Alabama!" He laughed and they shook hands again. He showed them around the classroom and library and the playing field in back. Through a grove of trees and wild flowers was a dormitory perched on a hill.

A number of students were lounging around waiting for lunch. A country record was playing. The director made the sort of fuss over Mom that she always enjoyed and said Cathy was welcome to visit the dorm any time.

"You'll see, you'll find lots of friends here," Mom said on the way home.

She never seemed to understand that friends never come in *lots*.

It was hard to concentrate on homework when you were waiting for the mail. There had been plenty of time for Pippa to get a letter here. Hadn't there? Her own notes counted the days.

> Tangier, AP8
>
> Cathy is busy with homework so asked me to write again. Yesterday afternoon she went riding, and a dumb new girl tried riding Tarik and fell off. The riding master said he should have known better.
>
> Mom had a big tea yesterday for American wives. Tonight she and Dad are having a big cocktail party for all American Personnel and the Diplomatic Corp. Cathy will wear a long dress and help pass sandwiches the way she did with you. She wishes you were here, but says to tell you she expected a letter before now. Every day she asks, "Any mail?" But every day there is no mail.
>
> Big Baaaaaaaa,
> BOOTS

Mom suggested that Rajah and Ouatif come over after school. They were polite and shy at first, but amazed when they saw Boots. Rajah asked, "Is this the one I gave?" as if she would like him back. Mom made a great fuss over them and helped them make cocoa, American style.

Tom loved the school and began having a good time right away. He was excited about a basketball game with the Spanish school. The coach said he was "excellent material" and would probably make the team next year. Already, after a few weeks, he had a whole bunch of buddies. Dad and Mom beamed.

But they were both nervous when Cathy kept asking about the mail.

"Is it coming through all right?"

"Of course."

"I mean *ordinary* mail, not the Bag." The diplomatic mail pouch came by special courier.

That seemed to be coming too.

"When is Pippa's mother coming back?"

Mom looked nervous. "I called, Cathy. Nobody seems to know."

AP12

Dear Pippa,

Cathy and Boots came in to see Dr. Prescot today. Boots has gained one pound three ounces. I didn't pay much attention to them because a woman in a terrible flowery hat with a dead bird on it brought in a horrible cat who came right up the wall after me. I was frightened half out of my feathers, but anyway *I* have gained half an ounce.

Love,
Little Owl.

P.S. Today in the *International Herald Tribune* there was a picture Cathy cut out for you. These five young screech owls were found abandoned and taken to a bird hospital in Fort Lauderdale, Florida. I am glad there are bird hospitals in the USA. Dr. Prescot said that down in Fez there is a special hospital for sick storks that you and Cathy can visit on your trip next summer.

Big Peck!
Little Owl

Two weeks. Pippa must have decided to send her a whole diary-letter at once, with her mother. Her mother must be coming soon or Pippa would have mailed it herself. She telephoned the secretary at the British Consulate.

"Could I speak with the Consul-General, please?"

"I'm sorry, he flew to London yesterday."

"When do you expect him back?" She knew the lingo, and she knew the secretary too, a stunning black-haired girl named Genevieve, from Australia.

Now Genevieve said, "Is this Cathy Scott?"

"Yes. I wondered when Pippa's mother is coming back. She's bringing me some things from Pippa . . ."

There was a little silence. "I see. I'm sorry, Cathy, but I really don't know." A still longer pause. "I could call you the moment we find out."

"Will you? Oh, *please*."

As she hung up, Cathy felt a wave of dread go over her. Pippa was sick. So sick that her father had to fly to England to see her. And who wouldn't be sick, alone at school with your mother going off any minute?

Pippa could have mailed two weeks of reports by now—but what did she really have to report? Poor Pippa! She had no Boots to weigh. No Little Owl. No Tarik. Nobody at all that Cathy knew. No Dr. Prescot to go and see. No Wool Woman. Pippa had described her narrow dormitory bed. She didn't even have a room of her own. No voices at night. No secret tree she could watch from. No friend. Sadly, Cathy looked at the letter she had just finished:

AP14

Dear Pippa,

Yesterday Cathy came to the riding school. This girl who is such a rotten rider rode on me again. She pulled too much on the bit.

The wild cistus is coming out now. It makes the hills look like green cloth with white polka dots. One of the English teachers at the American School is a very good rider. Cathy and Habiba rode with him clear to the high rocks and saw three ships on the Straits. It was quite misty, which made them look like Flying Dutchmen. No Gib in sight. No sign of Spain.

Cathy says to tell you that if you don't send her a letter soon I'm to bite you when you come back.

Love,
Tarik

Reading this herself gave her a feverish feeling. And the postscript was worse.

P.S. *Cathy brought me some sugar and we talked about you while Habiba and I were drinking.*

Big Nuzzle,
T.

Letters like that would kill me if I was homesick, she thought. And they had seemed such a good idea at first. Now she wrote;

Dear Pippa,

   This is Cathy. I know now that you are sick and I'm terribly sorry and I do understand how it is. But I feel sick too when I don't get a letter or any word at all. Could your mother or somebody just send me a card? Or your father could bring it, if he comes sooner.

   Boots is fine.

She wondered whether she should even mention him, but decided that it would be worse if she didn't than if she did. She went and weighed him and found he had gained nothing since the last time.

But he is losing weight because he misses you and because he is worried too.

   This stationery is quite special and I wouldn't use it for anybody but you. The horses in the pictures are Morgans, American horses that are very special. When you visit me in Washington (we always stay there for a while between postings), we'll ride two great Morgans I know on a farm that belongs to one of Mom's friends. It's near the Blue Ridge Mountains of Virginia, which is one of the most beautiful places in the world. Especially in the spring and fall. I love it in winter too, though, when snow is on the trees and bushes; it always melts first on the bridle paths. If you come in summer we can go to a point-to-point. There you'll see how Morgans run.

   They have a great history I can send to you. It was published in 1857 and is by a man named Linsley and is called *Morgan Horses*. The sire of the whole strain was called Justin Morgan after his master. He was a dark bay and was only fourteen hands high. You'll laugh when I tell you that Boots reminds me of him in one way—see, he had black legs, mane, and tail. Notice this description in the book when you read it, especially about his super muscles. He could pull as well as run.

There's a lot about Morgans in American history. It was a Morgan named Rienzo that General Sheridan rode in the Civil War; I've actually seen him in the Smithsonian War Museum. Pioneers took Morgans west: they were so sturdy they could pull wagons and ploughs. And they went to the Gold Rush and Brigham Young took one to Utah. I'll send you a poster of a western horse that I've had in my room for years but don't have space for here. It's a *cowboy* Morgan, cutting steers. I wish I could take you to a rodeo.

One of the nicest things—I remembered just now something about Morgans I'd forgotten until I started to really think about them for this letter. The big Morgan breeding farm is in New England (I like America having a *new* England) at the University of Vermont, where they first started, and the director there says he's sure Justin Morgan had *Arab blood*. How do you like *that?*"

Now she signed her own name. Her own "Love." And like Lily, a Big Kiss.

"Cathy," Mom said, "there's a dance this weekend at the dorm. The director called and asked us to come. Especially. Won't that be nice?"

"I don't want to go. I've got lots of homework."

"Not on the weekend. Please, Cathy, don't be like

that. You can't just mope around watching for the mail!"

Cathy flushed. Mom flushed. It was all too familiar. Once it had been Carol's letters that seemed to take forever getting from Washington to Bangkok.

"The other night at the party I had a little talk with your English teacher," Mom said.

Cathy turned away. I knew they were talking about me, she thought, when I was passing the sandwiches around. She could always tell. "I've done all of the homework he assigned," she said. "And I've read all the books on his stupid list already. So what did he have to say?"

"He said you were doing good enough work but you won't pay attention in class, you just sit there writing. Now, Cathy, for heaven's sake don't get this wrong and think he's been telling on you—or that I've been telling things, either—" because Cathy was now looking at her accusingly. "We both want to help you, that's all. Starting in mid-year in a new school is hard, we both know it."

"It's not hard for me. Most of the Moroccan kids are *dumb*. They can't even *talk* real English, let alone *write* it."

"Then you should try to help them, don't you think? They need conversation practice. Some of them want to get scholarships in America and they need a good command of English." It was all terribly familiar. Now she was supposed to limp along making talk with all those kids. "So I do think, Cathy, you should be glad to go to the dorm parties. It'll be a help to them and a help to you." More familiar still, Cathy thought it made her feel tired to listen. "In our position, we owe it to the community . . ."

She was in the middle of a letter to Pippa right now and needed to finish it to get it off in time for today's mail. "Okay," she said, starting off. "When is this messy dance?" She felt and looked like a horse pawing to get onto the path.

"Saturday. I'll have Latifa press that nice yellow dress."

As Cathy disappeared, Mom thought of what the teacher had said. And the Headmaster. Very understanding, both of them. Cathy seemed, they agreed, to be rather unpopular. She was so cold and distant with people. It might be that she was using her position in the community as the Consul-General's daughter not to help others, but to escape responsibility for herself. Very bright, they said, extraordinarily clever at writing, obviously. But one of the loners. It was very difficult with such children, to get them to take part.

"What can we do?" Mom had asked, feeling helpless. "Do you think she could be given a part in the school play, maybe? I hear you're doing one this term. She was in a play at her school in Washington and did very well."

"The play is only for high school students. Next year, a good idea."

And then the English teacher had a very good this-year idea. "If she would get acquainted with some of the bright students in the dorm, there are three of them very much involved in the school literary magazine this semester. She might contribute to that, and—"

"Oh, dear, more writing!" Mom said.

"No, they could ask her to help edit, that sort of thing. We do feel that if she worked with other students and got acquainted—"

"Oh, yes, I see that."

"Bring her to the dorm party and we'll see they all get together."

If she would only *try,* Mom thought. This awful news about Pippa . . . When Dad came for lunch she said, "I almost wish she hadn't met Pippa, after all. It seemed such a lucky thing at the time, and now . . ."

"I know," he said. "Poor kid." But he didn't mean poor Pippa, he glanced toward Cathy who was leading Boots onto the terrace for his bottle. Cathy had learned, watching sheep in the fields, how to hold the bottle like a mother's teat, and Boots would tug away with his bottom in the air and his rear gyrating like a belly dancer. It even looked a little obscene, he thought.

"I'm glad Pippa insists that she tell Cathy herself," Mom said. "I doubt I'd have the courage to do it, but I hope she'll do it soon."

It was raining again. Spring had grown dismal as if the weather reflected Cathy's black mood. But at last, one day after school, she saw the big black British limousine standing inside the gate.

Mom and Mum were having tea. When she came in they stopped talking instantly, the way parents always do when they have been talking about you. Before she could speak Mom said, "Darling, you're *sopping.* You'd better change *right now.*" But she had to know. She stood clutching her bookbag, and the two of them sat looking at her.

"Did you bring a letter from Pippa?" She asked. Point-blank, without even saying a first hello.

"Yes—and a gift she said was very special." Pippa's mother wasn't really smiling. "She simply loved the animal letters, Cathy. She's been in bed with some sort of flu. I really felt guilty to leave her."

Cathy stood staring at her. She looked so uncomfortable, so stiff and strange. Something terrible was wrong. Something worse than the flu. A horrible flash went through her mind: *Pippa has died.* She reached blindly behind her for a chair and sat down.

Pippa's mother foraged in her purse and brought out a big manila envelope. "She worked on this until the last possible moment," she said. And it came to Cathy that this was like one of those horribly important papers in a story—a will, a treasure map, a letter delivered after a soldier has died in a war. She reached for it.

"Goodness, Cathy," Mom said, "you *might* say thank you!" As Cathy ran out she called after her, "And get those wet clothes off before you do anything else— hear?"

Cathy did not hear. She sat on the floor and ripped the envelope open. A bundle of letters. They were tied together with a ribbon on which Pippa had lettered in embroidery, BOOTS.

My dear friend Cathy,

I wanted to write at once but I caught a cold and felt simply awful. For a few days I didn't care whether I even got better. That was mostly because of something Mum told me on the flight to London. I made her promise to see that nobody told you until I had a chance to write to you. I *had* to tell you myself.

The man who was our ambassador to Turkey was drowned, and my father has been posted there to help. He has to leave Tangier almost at once, Mum says. They didn't tell me before I left because they thought I felt bad enough already. I got them to promise that I could come back for a while when school is out and they're going to see if your parents will take us on the trip to Fez, instead. Otherwise I think I would have *died*. Oh, I hope your mother and father say yes.

And I might have died anyway without your reports from the animals, I was so sick. I think writing letters from Boots and Little Owl and Tarik is the cleverest thing I ever heard of. Please keep on with them. I read them to some of the girls and they think you must be simply brilliant. As you really are. One called Rose said she was surprised you were an American!!!!!!

The only really good thing for me to think about is our trip in July. I know it will be all right —we *will* go. It will be terribly hot in Fez that time of year, but after all there isn't any choice, as I told Mum. She really does understand how I feel, I think. Her father was in the Royal Navy and they moved a lot too and sometimes she didn't see him for months and months when he was at sea.

I keep trying to think of when we'll be eighteen and can do as we like.

As if he knew all about everything, Boots began a pitiful maaaaing from the terrace. He had got wet in the rain. He had nibbled at every single little shoot of green he could reach. Now he wanted milk and bunted against her when she let him in as if he thought she was an old baggy ewe. She pushed the letter back into the envelope with the others. Now she could wait to read the mail. The two women were talking in the hall as she started for the kitchen, waiting to see how she was taking the news.

"I'm frightfully sorry, Cathy. We feel miserable about this, all of us. It's so *tiresome*. But your mother and father have agreed to take you and Pippa to Fez, since we can't."

Cathy did not answer. She simply nodded and walked by as if she didn't care.

"As soon as I'm unpacked I'll send over the present from Pippa." Pippa's mum added.

Mom said, "Cathy, you didn't change out of those wet clothes . . ." but she was already out of sight on her way to the kitchen. Back in her own room, she fed Boots and dried him with a towel and brushed him fluffy. Then she lay down on the floor, staring up at a balloon globe Tom had given her for a long-ago birthday. He kept one of his own over his bed, and she remembered him telling her, "This world is a picture of my *home*."

In her mind she was telling Pippa this. But the world was not a cozy home where you could go into your own room and close the door. Mom felt happy lately because she had started to work with the kids at school. They were nice kids, interesting and smart. But she didn't want to choose any one of them to really know. This one semester would soon be over, and they'd scatter to Ghana and Nigeria and the States and India and a dozen other places. Some might come back, but they might not. Most of them didn't even know yet where they were going.

Strung from the ceiling on a string, the globe turned slowly and gently one way and the other.

"Cathy!"

She pretended not to hear. Mom came to the door. "Please, Cathy, get into some dry clothes. Why don't you take a shower and try to relax?"

"Okay," she said and turned slowly over onto her knees and hands. It always drove Mom absolutely crazy when she pretended to be an animal the way she had done since she was a little girl.

Mom said chattily, pretending not to notice what she was doing, "It isn't all bad, is it? You and Pippa will have that exciting trip together."

Cathy rocked from side to side; that used to be an elephant.

"Why on earth do you *do* that?" Mom asked nervously.

"It's an exercise. I *told* you." She went on rocking until Mom went away. Then she folded her legs under her and read Pippa's letters. She especially liked one part about school: "I hate every girl here. Nobody really wants to hear anything about Morocco; they just want to talk about what *they* did and where *they* went during the holidays, even if it was nowhere but Brighton."

Cathy knew how that was. When she went back to the States it was the same. Anyway, most of the kids she knew in Washington had been traveling around all their lives, and she didn't particularly want to know about their places, either. The important thing in the

States was to catch up on the TV shows and the best new records and get some exciting new posters for her room. There were always some new words to find out about, too; they weren't in dictionaries yet so you couldn't look them up.

Boots bunted at the door and she let him in. He had left a lot of his odd little pellets on the terrace and she went out to sweep them up. She heard a car drive up, out front, and the bell rang. Then Mom came back.

"They've sent over Pippa's present, Cathy. A book, I imagine."

She stood waiting for it to be opened. The package was tied with another of Pippa's pretty ribbons. Cathy smoothed it out and slowly unwrapped the book, folding the paper carefully.

"Good heavens, Cathy, you're usually in such a hurry to open a present!" Then, seeing it at last, Mom said, "Oh, it's the one about the otter. They made such a good film out of that, remember?"

Ring of Bright Water. Inside, Pippa had tucked another letter. Cathy sat looking at it and finally Mom had the sense to disappear.

This is my absolute favorite of all the books in the world. If you've read it already, it doesn't matter, I've read it at least ten times. Maxwell has been my favorite author for ages. He wrote a book about Arabs, too, not Moroccans but some who live in south Iraq. I've told Mum to get it from my room and give it to you to read. There's a wonderful scene about an eagle owl dying. The terrible thing about loving animals, he says, is that they always die so much sooner than people do and we have to bear it. He hated schools too; he had to go from one to the other, just the way you said you did, never having any real friends. Except animals. I had just been reading that book the day I heard about Foxy. The first day you came to tea, remember.

Write what you think about these books, please. And *please* don't stop the animal letters. They are the only really important things that happen to me here.

Mom said when Cathy disappeared immediately after dinner, "She's reading the book Pippa sent. Of course, an animal book."

"Very nice," Dad said.

"Yes, *very* nice. But she won't do another thing until it's finished."

"She doesn't do much else anyway, does she?" Dad asked. "I wish you'd remind her that she's supposed to be friendly with the natives."

Tom grinned. "Woops, Dad, you're always telling *us* never to call people 'the natives.' " Among the things never to do was to use words that might make people feel you regarded them as inferiors.

"We never do *in front of them,*" Mom said. But then she blushed, realizing that Latifa was just then bringing a pot of coffee and hearing everything. When she had gone back to the kitchen, Mom said, "One thing I like about going back to the states is being on our own—no servants to worry about."

"And all I hear when we get there is how hard it is to get along without help," Dad reminded her, laughing.

She looked pained. "How did *this* tired old discussion start?" she asked.

Cathy sat reading with her fingers moving through Boots' wool, around his neck, under his collar. She wished he would curl up and nestle and not be so jumpy. But after all he was not a cat. She remembered how wiggly Foxy had been when he was a puppy.

There was no choice. Boots had to go out if she wanted to read. Or write.

Dear Pippa,

Cathy has just pushed me out of the house so she can read a book about an otter. She thinks it is wonderful and will probably read it ten times the way she did a corny old book called *Heidi*. It's about goats and you know how impossible *they* are. They eat everything in sight and never leave so much as a leaf or a blade of grass for useful beasts like me. The Wilderness and Ecological Societies are all saying that goats *have to go*.

Cathy says to ask you if you have a copy of *Heidi* or should she send you one.

Her mother says sheep's milk has doubled in price since the natives knew we needed some. She is going to ask Dr. Prescot how soon I can be weaned. I already have some good nibblers. The gardener Assad took a fit this morning because I reached my nose under the wire and rooted up some pansy plants.

I tried following Cathy to school like Mary's lamb, but they wouldn't let me in. They said I was a distraction.

It rains every single day here and everything

looks sloppy. It is odd how good the weather was when you were here. Sunshine every day!

Now Cathy thought of it, it had rained several days when Pippa was here. She had not cared then, or even noticed much. Which said all there was to say, really, about the importance of weather. . . .

She made a design around the envelope with red and green ink. Now it should have a pretty Moroccan stamp, but she had no more. "Come on," she said to Boots, "help me mail your letter to Pippa." He followed along, his hooves clicking on the pavements. As always, people watched and smiled, and some children ran alongside. Today there was no official guardian at the post office, but there was, as always, a boy handy. One nudged her elbow and said, "Me, *me guardia!*"

She dug into her leather pouch and showed him a ten-franc piece. He said "Ee-yeá," which she knew was Moorish for "Yes" and then, grinning, said "Okay!"

She had to stand quite a long time in a "queue," which was Pippaese for a long line of people, to get the stamps. But she found especially nice ones, one of red poppies and one of a bright bird. There were others with pictures of broken stones called geodes which were like bowls of colored jewels. She bought a few of each. Every single one of Pippa's letters must be a work of art.

Outside again, a bigger crowd had gathered on the sidewalk, admiring Boots' white wool and ribbon and polished hooves. The boy was holding onto Boots' neck and called "*Shof! Shof!*" to Cathy as she appeared. Somebody else cried "*Regard! Regard!*" which she knew was the way the French say "Look!" Now she saw why: on either side of Boots' head was the beginning of his horns. Hard little buds deep in the wool. The boy waggled his fingers on either side of his own head, laughing, and half a dozen children followed her as far as the square. Like a parade.

So at once there was something else to report to Pippa. Later she took Boots over to the clinic to show Dr. Prescot. He got out the big book about sheep and showed her a picture of a Scottish Blackface and a Welsh Mountain Ram. "He will develop long curling horns, something like these," he said.

Suddenly she remembered that horrible day when she saw such horns on a head with glazed eyes. Eyes glaring at its own blood running into the gutter.

"I wish Boots would stop growing now," she said. "I wish he'd stay just this nice size, the way Foxy did."

Dr. Prescot touched her shoulder with a kindly hand. "That's impossible, you know. You are asking Nature to change her ways."

When she got home, Assad was asking the same. But angrily. He had found more of Boots' nibbling ruination in his flowerbeds. Mom said, "We must find a place where Boots can be taken care of—"

"Not yet!" Cathy cried.

"No—not *quite* yet." But Mom sounded helpless. "You must keep him inside his fence. And you promised to keep his clutter swept up, remember."

"He doesn't really make messes."

"Not soft and nasty like a cat. But he doesn't care where or when, does he? If just once more your father brings guests onto the terrace where Boots has been . . ." Later Cathy heard her talking on the telephone.

"Dr. Prescot called," Mom said at dinner. "He says

we might take Boots out to the Rest Home. His man Allal out there has a little flock of his own."

Cathy cried again, "Not *yet*—he's still so little—"

Mom was using her practical voice. "I was thinking of the future, and so was the doctor. We can't take Boots on our trip, after all. Can you imagine him left here alone with Assad?"

The torn feeling was familiar. There was nothing to do. So she gave Boots a bath and marveled at how white his white and how black his black.

One day she came home after school to find the Wool Woman visiting with Mom. "I have had a letter today from my friend Pippa—"

An odd jab of jealousy made Cathy turn her eyes away. She felt Lily studying her in an uncomfortable way. "Pippa reminds me that you like very much her small prayer rug."

Cathy looked up. "Yes," and remembering its thickness her fingers curled at her sides. "It's nice and thick, like Boots' wool."

"The skins in the bazaars—you see them everywhere—are well tanned. But they are dead, no? To me it seems the small *tapis* are still alive. From many sheeps, still warm, you see?"

Mom smiled. "What a nice idea," she said.

Lily sounded very firm. "Pippa says you must have a prayer rug of your own. But you must *make*—there must be in it your own hands."

Oh, dear. Cathy glanced at Mom and saw that she had lifted her eyebrows in a way she had when she was in doubt or surprised. "I'm afraid Cathy isn't very good at making things," she said. "Not enough patience."

"Then," Lily said firmly, "patience must be learned."

Cathy could see that Mom felt nettled by this positive woman. "I couldn't agree more," she said. "But if you have children of your own, you know it's easier said than done."

Cathy felt hot. She remembered Mom saying over and over, "If only you would paint—or sew—or learn to play an instrument . . ."

"Alas, no," Lily was saying, "I have no children. So it is that I may advise my sister and my friends who do."

Cathy's voice was louder than she intended. "I'm sure I can learn. Pippa said she learned and it was easy."

"The *easy* will come after the *learning*," Lily said. "And now could I make, please, the acquaintance with this famous lamb?"

As she led Lily down the stairs and to her room and its terrace, Boots began to bleat. "He hears me the minute I get home," she said. "Just like Foxy. Dad says he's too clever to be a lamb, he must be a *pup*." How much could be told to this woman who seemed quite different from other grown-ups? She plunged, for after all Lily was Pippa's good friend: "Pippa and I decided that maybe Foxy's spirit went into Boots when he was born. We read a story about a man's spirit going into a baby when he was killed in the war. So he became his own son!"

Lily smiled. "Some believe these things, some do not. I believe sometimes, sometimes not. But one must really believe another strange thing—surely animals have spirits as men do."

"But naturally!" Cathy cried. And Boots made another quavering maaaa as if to underline the fact now and forever.

"Boots, this is Lily." And Cathy added, laughing, "The Wool Woman."

Lily leaned down and ran her fingers through the thickening softness of Boots' neck. "It will be a long time before there is wool enough for spinning a single spool," she said. "But the real reason I have come is in Pippa's letter. You must read before we make an arrangement." She foraged in her big fat bag. "When she was here at first, she had no friends for a long time, only old ones like me who were not of much use, after all. She came to the Kasbah with her mother one day and became fascinated. So now she remembers and wishes for you the same. And why not? For me, it is very agreeable." she said it in the nice French way, *très agréable*.

Cathy took the letter eagerly. She and Lily and Boots sat together on the terrace while she read it. The important part came toward the end:

> Cathy wants a prayer rug like mine. You remember how much it helped me to work with wool when I was so lonesome. It would help her too. I'm sure her mother will think it's a good idea. Cathy said the doctor in Washington kept telling them she should *do* things like handwork for *therapy*. We laughed about it, but I do remember that

working on my rug made me feel a lot better. So I hoped you might teach her the way you did me."

"I wish I could come *today*," Cathy said.

"Today is finished there in the Kasbah and I have much else to do. But *tomorrow?*"

A little after dawn Lily arrived as she had promised on the telephone the night before. She was driving a small blue beetle. "He is thirteen years old—more than your age," she said, "and has done much work in the world already." They went straight down to the Grande Socco, which was already swarming with people and animals. Now Cathy saw the Wool Market Pippa had talked about.

It was in a huge cobbled courtyard off a narrow street. Along every wall and in lines in the center as well, women sat on the ground. Some wore veils and woolen *djellabas* with hoods over their heads. Others were unveiled, Berbers, with bright red-and-white skirts and beach-towel shawls and huge hats ringed with colored tassels. All of them sat with spread laps spilling over with shanks of wool.

"All is spun from her own sheeps by each woman," Lily said. Her assistant, Si Absolom, was already there and took her to see several of the choicest bunches. They must wait to buy until a signal was shouted by a master, a kind of auctioneer.

"*Feel,*" Lily said, and Cathy leaned shyly to run her fingers through a shank as white as Boots. "You see, tight and soft, well-spun. In time one learns good from bad—you see?" Suddenly there was a clamor and other buyers began to move also along the lines. Everybody seemed talking at once, gesturing, arguing. When Lily nodded, Si Absalom threw a big bundle of wool over his arm. Lily talked to the woman and wrote something in a notebook.

"I have told her the price is high, but the wool is good. They learn soon that excellent work means an excellent price. So I pay."

Later she had several arguments as they moved down the courtyard, and Cathy saw what dirty, ill-spun wool could be like. Lily even leaned down to smell now and then, wrinkling her nose. The pile of wool grew high in Si Absalom's arms.

"Is all this for *my* little rug?" Cathy asked, amazed. She could see why it would take many years for Boots to produce so much, if he *ever* could in a long life.

By the gate were two old men who looked like the disciples in Cathy's illustrated Bible. They sat on mats and before them were balancing scales. They bundled each woman's wool on one brass bowl and balanced it on the other with circles of metal that shone like gold, of various sizes.

"Each day we are told the price of a kilo of wool. It is much mathematics," Lily said, biting her pencil and writing in her book. The women whose wool had been chosen waited in a row. Each one knew her own wool perfectly well, in all that pile. Si Absalom paid them one by one with coins from a leather pouch.

Lily had bought a good deal of white and some off-white, dark brown and black. "Black is more rare, and I must buy in the time it is here," she said. The women smiled and nodded and seemed happy with the coins in their pockets.

In the back seat of the little beetle, Si Absalom seemed drowned in melly wool. "Wait—all this work has made me hungry," Lily said and rushed off to one of the stalls on the square where dough was cooking in huge kettles of boiling oil. She came back with a dozen cakes called *churas* in a square of heavy paper along with three small cartons of milk. Cathy had never tasted anything more delicious and ate all the while they climbed up to the Kasbah.

"Now the wool must be washed," Lily said. "While is drying, you will see how the loom is warped. There is a saying that a weaver must warp her own loom, for the spirit of her work grows into the threads."

It was so difficult and complex a task that two girls and Si Absalom did most of the work, winding string from a huge ball onto two pegs, crossing it each time it was stretched from one to the other. When all this was lifted onto the loom it seemed a wonder that it was not hopelessly tangled, but soon it was neatly set, as even as the strings of a harp. Mysteriously half of them rose, half fell, and shuttles were sent flying through.

"You will see soon how it goes. Now it is time for lunch," Lily said. "Tomorrow we will work hard. The *learning* before the *easy*."

The wool felt alive in her fingers. She sat on a small stool before the loom where two Moroccan girls were working. For a time she watched and Lily asked them to work slowly. A thread passed between two warps on the loom and was turned about and brought into a knot which slid firmly down against the threads below. It seemed terribly awkward and difficult, especially holding the scissors for clipping in the right hand at the same time the hand was supposed to be tying. The girls laughed at her when she put the scissors down each time. They showed her again and again. When a full row of knots had been tied a thread was run across and it was all pounded firm with a sort of iron comb.

Lily said, watching, "Let them be happy laughing at you. It is not very much they have that is better than a rich American girl."

She spoke to them in Arabic and they looked pleased. "I have told them they are my best girls, your own age. They wish very much that you learn to do good work." When she had gone away they helped once more, giggling but patient and kind. When Cathy finally began to make every knot properly, firm and even, holding the scissors, they called other girls to see.

If only she could talk to them! She asked Lily for some more learning. "First I want to say thank you," she said. This turned out to be a marvelous word. "There was a famous faithful servant of Mohammed," Lily said, "whose name was Baraka. So it came to be the word for a good spirit, and *Barakalofic* came to mean thanks."

Barakalofic. "And when you say it you might show good feeling as well. Moroccans are very fond of candy. If you should bring along a small bag of peppermints . . ."

The next afternoon Cathy was a huge success at the loom. They all laughed and sucked candy and sang songs which they began to teach her as well. Her fingers grew more clever every day.

Dear Pippa

Thanks a million times for arranging for me to make the little rug. I am going almost every day after school to work on it, and I'm getting pretty good at the knots. I'm determined to have it finished before you come. Then we can carry our rugs with us on The Trip. I always put The Trip in capital letters in my mind. Do you? Even though sometimes it seems to me that the end of The Trip will be The End of the World.

Working knots I almost never think of unpleasant things. Lily says that Making is to be happy, and I am sure it is true. Today she told me about a friend of hers, a famous American weaver named Sheila Hicks. From the time she was a little girl she noticed spiders weaving. She says webs are *structures*, threads organized and arranged. I looked up *spiders* in the encyclopedia just now. And then *spin*, because *spin* is from a very old English word, *spinnan*, to draw out like the threads from a spider. Spinning and weaving are the oldest arts of all. I had never thought about this before, even when I saw ancient skeletons in museums and could see the threads of the cloth they were wrapped in. In India they weave cloth so fine that one pound of cotton makes a thread nearly 253 *miles* long! Just imagine!

I'm supposed to write something for our school literary magazine and I'm thinking about writing on weaving. The mag is called *Al-Tanjaoui* which means *The Tangerine*.

I read about Oriental carpets and how the

frames for weaving are strung like harps. But a harp has nineteen strings to each foot of width, and a loom has from ninety-six to seven hundred twenty! I remember looking at the silk looms in Bangkok and it makes my head spin to think of how many threads there are on those. How on earth do they do it? I'm glad I'm working with nice thick wool or making my little rug would take the rest of my life.

Something interesting happened in the Kasbah yesterday. Some men came in to talk to Lily about some new rules in Morocco now that are supposed to give work to more people. Every business run by outsiders—Europeans and Americans mostly—has to have some Moroccan people to help run it. These men told Lily that she should buy some machines so rugs could be made faster and make more money. You would have loved the way she scolded them. If some people do not go on with the work of the hands, she shouted, it will disappear forever! Why must everything go faster and faster and nobody have *time for making?* Can't you just hear her? *The world is forgetting that the making is a way to be happy!*

I really do know now that this is true. My little loom is like a friend. I thought weaving might get tiresome but it never does. The girls are laughing and talking all the time and they are teaching me some Moroccan words. Did you find yourself tying knots in time to their singing? I do.

There is one Moroccan word that says something is good or beautiful or delicious. *Mezyan!* And the word for feeling happy and thankful is

Hamdulah! I say it whenever I think of you and The Trip and showing you how Boots is growing. It sounds like a combination of *Hallalujah* and *Hurrah,* don't you think?

Mom said, "How did the editorial meeting go today?"

Okay, I guess."

"But what *happened?*"

"Nothing."

"Isn't the time getting a little short for you to do nothing? I should think—"

"Well, I've been working on this poem. I'm supposed to hand it in by Thursday." And Cathy slipped away. In her room she added another note to Pippa's letter:

I have to write a poem for school. While I weave is the best time for thinking about it. When it's done I'll send it to you. I call it "The Loom of Friendship." It's the rhymes that are hard; I like poems with lots of rhymes, one at the end of every line. Do you?

Pippa wrote:

The book came. Thanks very much. Even if goats are a menace they must be awfully nice when they are babies. Like Boots. Heidi gave me an idea. If I got so homesick I walked in my sleep, they might get upset and send me home. So I tried it night before last. Once I was Lady Macbeth in some Shakespeare bits at school and got to be really good at sleep-walking. But all they did was send me to the infirmary. I had to sleep in a terrible hard bed with a fence around it.

Cathy wrote:

Here's a better idea; you could vomit. The thing to do is drink lots of soda and put your fingers down your throat where it tickles, right after you eat. . . .

Pippa wrote:

I tried the vomiting and it worked all right. But they gave me the most *ghastly* medicine and put me in that awful bed again with hot water bottles and a hideous smelly pot by the bed for me to be sick in. So quoth the raven, NEVERMORE.

I'm looking forward to the poem. Dad's got an old book called *The Loom of Youth* that's about school. Nothing about weaving, though, it's all boys and cricket.

Cathy wrote:

Mom insisted I invite the Moroccan girls to our place again. So Rajah and Ouatif came after school and I decided to invite Karen, too, that Voice of America girl you met at my birthday party. A girl named Valery whose father is Info Officer somewhere in Africa came too. She works on the school magazine and is quite smart.

We decided to organize a Club. We elected you a Member in Absentia and Boots is the Mascot. We are called the TILs, THE INTERNATIONAL LAMBS. Nobody but us will know what it means. I enclose your membership ribbon. Karen did the lettering. She's especially good at that, she does it for the school magazine. Guess our password—*Maaaaaaaaaaa!*

This is all pretty childish, I know, but Mom insists I have to do something with the girls because I am a Representative of the United States of America. We decided to meet at different houses —really Mom's idea—so I'll get a chance to get inside a real Moroccan house. Rajah lives on the Charf, that steep hill south of town by the old bull ring. Ouatif lives on Boulevard de Paris, but she says they are changing the name of the street now because a huge new mosque is being built on it. It will be Avenue Sidi Mohammed Ben Abdallah after the man who was Sultan of Morocco when Washington was president of the USA. We go to Ouatif's house next week and I'll tell you all about it.

Tom got a calendar for my desk that has everything in French. So on this calendar I've been figuring how many more days of my school and yours. Why do English schools have to go on until July? Our graduation day is June 19 so I decided to start a different kind of numbering on my letters that day. Instead of AP Time I'll start *B*efore *P*ippa Time. Then the numbers will get smaller and smaller until 6BP and there's no time to get a letter to you before you ARRIVE.

Lots of Love, a Monstrous Maaaa
and a Hearty Hamdulah!
Cathy.

P.S. Tom says Sultan Sidi Mohammed Ben Abdallah was the first world leader to recognize the new United States of America. So we have a strong link and these countries have always been good friends.

She enclosed a crushed pansy "for thoughts" but did not say that it was the only one left in one of the flower beds after Boots had a fine forage that afternoon.

Dad had come rushing in. "Cathy, Assad just came to talk to me. He says if that animal gets out *once more*—"

"Dad, I *promise*. See, I had him drying after his bath—there's no sun on my side in the afternoon—and I started to read . . ."

It was a very old story. "If you keep a pet, Cathy, you must take responsibility for it. Go right this minute and apologize to Assad."

Assad was digging angrily. He knew almost no English so Cathy asked Latifa how to say "I am very sorry" in Spanish, which he spoke very well. *"Lo siento mucho,"* she said to his bent back. He only grunted. So she went back to Latifa and wrote carefully, according to the sounds, *"Ela gristi bizef,"* which was Arabic as nearly as she could say it. He grunted again. She tried *"Je regrette beaucoup,"* thinking he might, like most Tangerines, know a little French. But only when she said it in English, very firmly, did it seem to *sound* very sorry and caused him to stand up and give her a little nod.

She fastened Boots to a tree with a leash but in a little while there was only a circle of bare ground as far as he could stretch it, while he made a wretched noise the whole time. She took him for a walk over a hill where she had seen a little grass. He kept his nose to the ground the whole time. She could carry grass from the countryside for him, she thought, the way she had seen Moroccans doing. She went to Dr. Prescot the next day for some of the barley mixture he had recommended. He said, hearing her problem, "It is sad, Cathy, but you cannot bring home all the grass he needs. I'm afraid you must take him to the meadows."

"Not until after Pippa comes!"

She told Mom and Mom told Dad. "Just before we leave for the trip Boots will go to the Rest Home the way Foxy used to go to the kennel."

"I remember a few bad scenes then," he said.

"I know," Mom said, "but it will be easier with Pippa here."

Dear Pippa,

I took my notebook to the Kasbah so I could write down my rhymes as I think them up. It's really lovely the way working with my *hands* makes my *head* go. The girls kept watching and whispering and Lily told them I wasn't "making magic" but making up a sort of song. They can't read, so they think it's odd to write songs down; they learn everything with their ears. Imagine! What on earth would we do if we couldn't read books—or write letters? It actually makes me sick in my stomach when I think about it—*not to read, ever*. What do they do in the night when they can't sleep?

Lily says that sometimes Americans and other people come to visit and say she is "exploiting

Moroccan children." She says they get "hot on
their collars" about "child labor" and don't seem
to believe that mothers and children come to her
off the streets, *begging* for work. There aren't
enough schools for them to go to. I asked Dad
about it tonight and he says it's really true. There
aren't even any books in the Moorish kind of
Arabic—schoolbooks are in classical Arabic which
is quite different from the kind ordinary Moroccans speak. Isn't that a *muddle?*

I am sending you a copy of *Al-Tanjaoui*. I
wrote "For Pippa" on my poem but they didn't
print it, so I've written it in. Tom says "chord"
and "word" don't really rhyme, and neither do
"wove" and "love" or "afterward" and "bird," but
I think it's the sound that matters, don't you? My
teacher said lots of good poets use half-rhymes,
especially Emily Dickinson. So sucks to old Tom-
Tom. Anyway, Dad and Mom were pleased.

The Loom of Friendship (for Pippa)

It seemed that I was fated
To live life like a warp
Of threads all separated
Like the strings of a harp.

There was no hand to bring
The notes into a chord,
Though now and then a string
Would vibrate at a word.

Then someone came who wove
Bright threads of laughter through,
The red and gold of love
But also lots of blue.

And ever afterward
The fabric was a charm
Like the feathers of a bird
To keep me nice and warm.

by Cathy Scott.

The girl who was editor of the paper was the brightest one in the whole school. She made some suggestions for my poem that were okay. But the oddest thing, when I told her I wished I could stay for years in the same school, she asked why. She thinks moving around is great and has been in *thirteen schools*. Quite a few of them were in the U.S.—her Dad is in oil. She says she just settles in and does things with the other kids and that there are always some nice ones wherever she goes.

Do you think I'm just too *choosy?*

Graduation was very nice and there were lots of prizes. Next year maybe I'll knock myself out and try for my class prize. It would give such a kick to Mom and Dad. Everybody cried, saying good-bye. It's strange to think how many of these kids will never in their whole lives see each other again.

Today I went to your house with Dad and Mom to talk to your mother about The Trip. Dad has to make reservations. Your things were mostly in boxes and I couldn't bear it, so I went out and lay in your tree. Everything looks the same except there are red and pink geraniums all over the walls and bougainvillea is blooming in masses. I heard donkeys braying from the fondouk and that same beggar was singing outside the wall.

Tom found a wonderful map to mark our route on. You know how he is, he's reading up on the places we're going. The trouble is, he says, we can't see the whole country in this one go. . . . Do you know what he said about you? He's glad you're going with us because you're "one girl at least with a brain." I was so pleased with what he said about you that I forgot until afterward to be insulted with what he meant about *me*. Anyway, boys never think their sisters amount to much.

In fact, this gave me a rather good idea. If Tom goes on being nice the whole trip and you like him, maybe in a few years you could marry him and then we would be sisters. It's the only possible way I can think of for us to be in the same family so we could go to all the same places the rest of our lives.

Two more inches of knots and I will be able to take my rug off the loom!!!!!!

Cathy

P.S. This is Boots. I am getting so heavy Cathy needs help to get me into the tub. Anyway Latifa took a fit so now I get washed under the hose, which I hate. The other day a kid at the post office stole my ribbon and I gave him a good *bunt*.

Boots
(His Mark)

She inked Boots' foot and made an imprint at the bottom of the page.

The next day Tom didn't appear until lunch. He had a roll of papers that he kept beside his plate. Important, Cathy could tell. She had learned that when he acted elaborately careless about something he had made it was apt to be special. But it was better not to ask.

Dad did, though, in a roundabout way. "What did you think of our itinerary? Did you make copies for all of us?"

Cathy sat up, excited. *Our itinerary.* The Trip. Tom said, "I marked a map. Got some Xeroxes at the office."

One was for Cathy, one for Pippa. She gave Pippa's a pale wash of colors, blue for the sea, green for the mountains, rust-red for the desert, not too heavy so the names of all the places were clear. Pippa would be pleased to see such a big fat letter:

> Tom made this map from the plans Dad's staff worked out for us. He may be awful in lots of ways but you'll see he's really great on a trip. He's found a lot of old Moroccan books here—they were given to the American Consulate by an American who used to live here. Tom says the best one will be more useful than a regular guidebook. It was written by an Englishman named Budgett Meakin. It's called *The Land of the Moors* and was printed in *1901!* This Budgett and his best friend rode all over Morocco *on bicycles.* Don't you wish we could do that instead of having to go in our big limousine with Official Guides leaping at us every time we stop?

"At Ouatif's house?" Mom looked pleased. Maybe, Cathy thought, organizing The International Lambs would turn out to be the best idea yet for making Moroccan friends. Ouatif seemed shy about having them at her house, as if she wondered whether it was grand enough. She took them far south of town where

Tangier was pushing out into suburbs. Her house was white, one of a row three stories high, all with doors and windows and balconies painted bright colors. The roof-tops were flat and on almost every one of them clothes fluttered in the wind.

It was disappointing that Ouatif did not live in one of the old thick-walled mysterious houses in the Kasbah. These seemed much like townhouses anywhere. But as soon as Ouatif opened the front door everything began to be different.

A whole family of women waited to greet her friends. Grandmother, mother, two little sisters, two aunts and some cousins were all dressed in brilliant caftans overlaid with gauzy flowered tops. The smallest sister, who could barely walk, was dressed in a silver robe with golden lace and looked like a decoration for a Christmas tree. Small gold earrings dangled from her pierced ears.

The old lady, tinkling with earrings and bracelets, led the way to a long room that had couches along every wall, lined with dozens of fat cushions. Patterned tiles were set into the wall as high as the girls' heads and all the floors were tiles, shining clean, scattered with sheep-skin rugs.

Now Ouatif beamed with pride. Her grandmother sat down on a hassock beside a huge bronze tray set on folding wooden legs. Almost at once a maid brought another large tray laden with bronze pots and gilded glasses. On her arms, too, were rows of bracelets that clinked musically when she lowered the tray. Now the girls could see how elegant the grandmother was, her gray hair coiled into thick braids with gilded combs, gold buttons all down the front of her dress. She wore embroidered silk slippers. She was the one to make the tea, and they all watched with fascination as she set to work.

It was as ceremonious, Cathy thought, as a Japanese tea she had once attended with Mom. A large bronze kettle of boiling water was brought and bright green leaves of fresh mint put into each glass. Into a teapot went tea leaves and lumps of sugar. The old lady poured and tasted and then, as a good cook always must, poured and tasted again. When she seemed satisfied that the tea was exactly right she poured it into the glasses which Ouatif carried to her guests on a smaller tray. The maid followed with two plates, laden with cakes, coconut cookies, hot glazed pastries, and candy that looked like peanut brittle.

Everything was delicious. Ouatif's mother beamed to see how much all the girls ate. Grandmother sat back with her eye on any glass that might need refilling and Rajah whispered to Cathy that it was polite to drink at least three glasses. When everybody had finished, Grandmother spoke. Ouatif listened, nodding, and then translated for the Americans what she had said.

"My grandmother is glad that Cathy and her family will go on a journey in Morocco. She would like to know to what places they will travel and where they will stop for the night."

If only she had brought Tom's map! Cathy tried to remember some of the names. "First we will go to Rabat where we hope to see the King's palace. Then Casablanca and Agadir and to the desert. We will come back through Marrakesh and . . ." she paused. What was the name of the old Roman city? "There is an ancient city that has been dug up—before Fez . . ." They would all know, of course, that Fez was the most important place of all.

"The Roman city was called Volubilus. It is near Meknes and Moulay Idriss." To Cathy's relief, Ouatif knew all about it and repeated the names to her grandmother. The old lady's smile made a map of long lines over her face, like the roads and rivers on Tom's map.

"She is sad you will not go to the place where she was born," Ouatif translated carefully. "It is called Ketama, in the mountains of the Rif. Her children were born in Al Hoceima northward on the sea." She listened again. "She says she knows people who suffered the earthquake in Agadir. A child has remained crippled since then and his poor mother died under many stones."

Again Grandmother murmured, sighing. "She says that you will not find the King at home in Rabat. He is coming soon to Tangier for a visit. It would be better, in any case, for you to see him here when he rides along this very street."

"When?" Cathy asked, excited. "My father heard he was coming sometime soon, but nobody knows exactly."

Nobody knows *exactly,* Ouatif's mother explained, because of wicked people from other countries who have slipped into Morocco and have tried, several times, to kill the King.

The old lady spoke again, in great excitement. Ouatif translated: "She says we will all know when the flags go up. My uncle arrived this morning and said they are beginning to hang them in towns along the road."

Then Grandmother said something that Cathy could tell was serious and important. Ouatif repeated it slowly, smiling. "She says it is good your English friend Pippa will travel with you. She says there is an old Moorish proverb: Before the road is chosen, it is wise to choose carefully—in order for the journey to be a happy one—the friends of the road."

Cathy felt, hearing these words, the splendid sensation that sometimes comes from seeing a beautiful thing, perhaps a sunset or a rainbow. Or from reading a perfect line in a book, especially a poem. How marvelous to write this to Pippa! She would say, "I have chosen my Friend of the Road."

Ouatif was saying, "Now you must all hear music and we will dance a Moorish dance." She took up a drum of decorated pottery and held it under her left arm while she began to tap rhythmically with her fingers. Her small sisters rose and began to move about the room, following her, giggling into their hands now and then. Ouatif's mother tied a scarf under her buttocks, bunching her dress behind, and danced with them, encouraging them with snaps of her fingers. Then even the old lady stood up and danced, her hands on her hips. Presently she too picked up a drum and one of the cousins played on a small flute. Rajah found a tambourine and kept time with the drums, and they all sang together. Ouatif's mother took Cathy's hand and drew her to her feet. Then Karen and Valery.

So they all danced. It wasn't long before they were following the beat of the drum, swaying and clapping and stamping. When they stopped to rest Rajah said,

"Moroccan women dance like this for weddings, and when their babies are born and when they're christened. For every great feast. For the King's Crown Day, for the end of Ramadan, and for Aid El Kabir. Sometimes we dance all night long."

Now, Cathy thought, she would know what was happening when she heard music in the night. Saying goodby, everybody kissed everybody. Cathy spoke for all the guests: "We think this was the best meeting *ever.*"

Ouatif blushed with pleasure. "Perhaps—after Pippa goes—you will come here many times."

Even though Cathy did not want to think about After Pippa, she had a strong good feeling. A Moroccan friend could tell her all the interesting things she needed to know here in Tangier. Today this seemed another kindly Act of Fate for a State Department Brat to cherish.

BP15

Dear Pippa,

Now that school is out and the gardener makes Cathy tie me up, she takes me for walks morning and night. Every day this week we have gone to see Dr. Prescot. Little Owl sends his love. When I asked whether I should say hello to Pippa, he asked, Who? Who? *Who?* though he knew perfectly well the whole time, of course.

BP11

I am handsome in the ribbon you sent. Cathy showed me to a lamb in a glass but he had a ribbon the same color as mine, so I gave him a good bunt and cracked him down the middle.

Dr. Prescot told us a good animal story about a man who brought a big boxer named Colonel to the clinic. This man's wife died and he was all alone and feeling sick and terrible. So when his neighbors had to go to India for a year they asked him to take care of this dog. Dr. P. said he used to be thin and pale and nervous with eczema all over his face and neck. But after he had this dog a few weeks he was like another man. His skin cleared up and he laughed and talked just the way he did when he was young. This was because he had somebody to take care of—and had to take him out for long walks five times a day.

BP8

Cathy says that without our walks she would probably break out with *boils* like Job. She works as slowly as she can on the prayer rug because she hates to finish it and have nothing to do in the Kasbah every day. Lily says she is glad she does not pay Cathy by the hour.

Big Kiss and Big Nibble,

Boots

When Cathy woke on the morning Pippa was to come, the first thing she saw was her grandma's sampler. *This is the day.* This, she thought, is what it means—to *rejoice.*

"Eat, Cathy. Don't fidget. You can't get that plane here any faster by fussing about it."

Beside Cathy's plate lay a sheet of paper she kept scribbling on. "You can wait until after breakfast to do that, can't you?" Dad asked.

"No. I have to figure. See, we've got six days to do all the things we were going to do *all summer*."

"That's rather silly, isn't it? Wait until Pippa gets here and then decide which you'd rather do."

She put the paper on her lap and finished eating. He couldn't be expected to understand that it wasn't what they'd rather do, but what they *had* to do. For the last time.

"Does Mohammed understand we have to leave early? We have to be there as the plane's coming in—I want to wave the two flags from the balcony."

"If he doesn't understand he must be as deaf as a post," Mom said.

"Did you tell Latifa that Pippa and her mother will be here for lunch?" Cathy really knew she had. She could see that even Boots understood what a special day it was. He was restless and sloppy, shaking at his ribbon as if he wanted to get it off. She wound her watch every half hour as if it needed winding. This is the day. This is the hour. This is the minute.

At last they were on the way. From the balcony at the airport she saw Pippa at once, the first one off the plane. Waving the flags wildly, she thought, *This is Now.*

Of course Boots was Number One on the list. Pippa hugged him, digging her fingers into his clean wool. "He's huge," she said, "but he remembers me."

"Of course. I've talked about you every day. And think of all those letters he wrote to you!"

They must take him for a walk; they must take him to see Dr. Prescot. And as always, the doctor knew just what to say. First, of course, "Welcome, welcome," and then, "Who would dream that three months ago this was a hungry bundle of bones?" During an exciting "weighing in," he was called to the telephone.

"Do you two want to go out with me? I have some patients in a village out in Bahraine, and now they say a colt's got himself tangled in a fence."

"That was one of The Things We Had to Do," Cathy said.

The Land Rover stood waiting in the street. "What about Boots?" Cathy asked in dismay. "Is there time to drop him off at home first?"

The doctor laughed. "Mustapha might be able to take care of one small lamb for a while," he said. "He has only seven donkeys, one egret, and a couple of storks to worry about today." As they drove away they were both sure they heard Boots bleating plaintively behind them. But riding high through the Tangier streets and then directly into the country, they forgot him. Tangier was growing in every direction, along the highways. Rows of flat-roofed houses were in every stage of construction along new dusty, rocky streets. In the middle of all this clutter was a village of shacks thrown together from flattened cartons and old cans. "The government is trying to get rid of these Bidonvilles," Dr. Prescot said. "But they go on and on making the worst mistake they could possibly make—their fine new housing for the poor has no places for families to keep a goat, a cow, a few chickens, or a little donkey. These people come from the country, they have no way of living without their animals. So they refuse to move."

The highway inland ran between ripening fields of millet and barley. Eucalyptus trees lined the road until a crossing that took them bumping onto a narrow road up a hill and over the top. On the edge of a village a small Arab house clung to a steep slope. Its thatch sloped to the ground on one side and there, inside the lean-to it formed, was a horse standing in a sludgy shade with a little colt teetering on muddy-bloody legs.

"Oh, dear," Pippa said, holding onto Cathy's hand as the owner led the mother out, lowering her head and sagging at the legs to get herself through the low entrance. The foal was puny and bony and wildly sweet and young. They both thought of long-legged Boots when he was new. He had to be held firm, despite his trembling, to have his wounds painted and to receive an injection from the doctor's long needle. By the time he had finished, a circle of Arabs all ages and sizes stood about watching, staring at Cathy and Pippa. They were glad to be in the high seat of the Land Rover again.

"Will he be all right?" Cathy asked. "That—the *shed*—" It couldn't be called a barn. "It was so little and dirty—"

"I've seen worse," he said, puffing on his pipe comfortably as they drove on the narrow road again. "I've delivered some healthy calves into a sea of mud and dung. It's home to them. Like the children, they've developed centuries of immunity to their own dirt."

Entering a rocky village he said, "This is where I once delivered a two-headed calf. People still mark time by great events out here in the country. Every now and then somebody says to me, 'That was the year Abdel-slam's cow had a two-headed calf.' "

"What happened to him?" Pippa asked, and then to Cathy's horror, "Could we see him?"

"No, he was dead when he was born. But he was famous anyhow."

When they stopped again on a small square of sloping grass around a well, a crowd was waiting with the owner of a cow heaving with pain. "It's too early for her to deliver," Dr. Prescot said, and the driver brought out the medicine box. It was fascinating to see him put on long thin rubber gloves and, while one of the boys held up the cow's dirty tail, feel up inside her to see where her calf was. His face was thoughtful and absorbed. "She'll be all right," he said, the driver repeating to the crowd every word. "Some indigestion—she's windy." And this cow, too, got a shot from the long needle, barely flinching when it went in.

A woman had appeared from an enclosure nearby leading a pair of young sheep, obviously twins. They had been sick, they refused to eat. And surely they were the saddest, thinnest, dirtiest creatures imaginable— compared with Boots. They too got medicine and the woman got advice. A calf appeared, a nervous dog, a child with a rabbit. Anybody could see that the doctor's visit was an event in which the whole village wanted to take part.

On the way out of this village he told them how it had been here in the beginning. Nobody ever helped a sick animal or expected others to help it. "All is the will of Allah!" they would say, and let it die. They had no right to interfere with anything that happened either to their animals or their wives and children. "But we found the right answer to *that*. It was Mustapha's idea. 'Yes, all is the will of Allah,' he would say, 'and it is Allah who has sent the doctor here to help.' They accepted this and now we always have an approving crowd wherever we go. We used to scout the markets and the roads for ailing donkeys but now they are brought to us. One pilgrim brought us a sick gazelle he had fetched all the way from Mecca."

Pippa looked proud; she already knew about these exciting things. "I'll show you the last report, Cathy," she said. "Imagine—altogether there were sixteen thousand cases treated by the PDSA last year."

"That's the whole lot—includes hamsters and white mice and tortoises," Dr. Prescot said.

"And storks," Cathy said, watching one circling above them. "And egrets." A flock of them had settled white around three grazing cows.

"I carry my binoculars with me. You never know when some different bird will turn up," the doctor said. He pointed out a bee-eater and a hoopoe, which were always around North Africa. "The migrators are mostly gone north by now; in the spring and fall we get some marvels. And that's when the boys go shooting and trapping."

A large bird with pointed wings circled over a field and plunged down. "A kite," he said. "A predator, that one, like the boys."

They took turns with the glasses. "Maybe that's where we get the name for the kites we fly," Cathy said. "It's *my* turn now, Pippa!"

"Of *course* that's where the name comes from." Pippa spoke as if she had been told something common that she had known forever. In about half a minute she said, "It's my turn now."

"Several times I've gone with my friends in Washington to a kite-flying contest on the Mall," Cathy said, shading her eyes to go on looking as the bird circled around and around. "I had one from Thailand that got a prize. It was exactly like a bird, like a flying peacock. And there was one man who had a kite so big he had to use an old bicycle, pedaling to put it into the sky."

"A *man?* I thought flying kites was for children," Pippa said.

Dr. Prescot turned his head to smile. They were getting a bit jumpy, he thought, and said, "Time to get back to work."

Just outside Tangier again, he pointed to an old house falling to pieces on a hill. "A real English Lady used to live there," he said, "in the old days when Tangier was full of spies and smugglers and all sorts of odd people. This Lady kept seventy-five dogs, thirty-three cats, seventeen parrots and twenty-eight horses. Once I figured out that, with other miscellaneous creatures, she kept a total number of three hundred and seventy-six!"

The girls had quieted down, and when they reached the clinic they clambered eagerly out to retrieve Boots. In the courtyard he was nowhere to be seen. The doctor said, "He's probably bedded down nicely with our new kid."

And there he was, sleeping in a pile of straw in the corner of a stall with a baby goat. "He manages to content himself wherever he is," Dr. Prescot said. "If we could do the same—"

"We're *humans,* not animals!" As soon as she spoke, Pippa's face went scarlet to think how it sounded. She looked quite unnatural with a scowl on her face. She held Boots fondly while Cathy straightened his collar and ribbon.

"I was thinking," Dr. Prescot said, "we might as well keep him here now, and tomorrow we could take him out to the Rest Home at Babana. We'll be taking the horse ambulance . . ." Seeing their dismayed faces he added rather hastily, "You're leaving on your trip in a day or so, anyhow."

"We've got *two more days!*" Cathy cried, but he raised his voice and finished what he had meant to say. "He's too big to go in a car, and I gather from your Mom, too messy besides."

"We were going to give him his nice blue bath *tonight.*" They did not look at him again or at each other.

"Of course, suit yourselves," he said. "He'd go easier in the ambulance."

They almost forgot to thank him for the nice trip before they escaped with Boots into the street. Several people were arriving with animals, and they knew several others were waiting. But they paid no attention to anybody but Boots.

"After all," Pippa said, sounding as if she had sucked at a lemon, "he's had sixteen thousand other patients this year—what's one lamb to *him?*"

"He talked just like a *parent!*" said Cathy.

Two parents saw them coming from the big front

window of the consulate. "Oh, dear, they didn't leave him," Mom said. "I especially asked Dr. Prescot—there's enough to do, getting ready and all, without having Boots to worry about."

Dad said, "I wish they'd stop talking about all these visits back and forth. Can you imagine packing Cathy up and sending her off alone to *Istanbul?*"

"Anyway, Lily always knows what's important," Pippa said the next morning as they went through the arch to the Kasbah. "You'd have thought Dr. Prescot expected us *not to care.*"

"We'll never hear that from our Wool Woman." They went in with their fingers twined together.

"So! Here the two together again!" A good beginning. "You will cut free your *tapi* now; then it is forever beside you." Yes, she would always say the exact right thing. As the warp was taken from the loom the ends dangled like uncombed hair. They sat on the floor to braid and tie the threads firm. "Not even a square meter there. But if somebody asked the price, what could be said? There is no price when the hands are in."

Lily went about her work and they sat collecting threads and making small braids, Cathy on one side and Pippa on the other. "I'm glad there is some of *your* hands in," Cathy said.

"I think your rug is nicer than mine," Pippa said generously. But added, "I was so much younger then."

"Only last year!"

"There's an *enormous* difference. And think how much difference the *next* years will make—we'll soon get to be what Mum calls 'Terrible Teens.' "

They worked in comfortable silence, as only good friends can do. Cathy knew the workshop sounds well now—singing and chattering and pounding and whirring of shuttles. And Lily talking in different languages to the girls, to the men, and to visitors from France and Spain and Norway and everywhere. Today there were two young architects from Germany and a decorator from Zurich, all loud and eager with ideas.

They were almost finished when Lily came back to them. "These people," she said, "who love the wool and the work of the hands, they must come to the old countries to find. A backward third-world country, Morocco—so the professors say. But what is backward? Working with the hands, living with the animals?"

They smiled at each other, pleased.

"But even in this place—it is no more the same. The young—they will not want to do it more. It is the old who come down to the markets bringing their making." She leaned down and ran her fingers through the thick rows of tight knots Cathy had tied during all these weeks. "And the old will die soon. Then—?" She gave a great sigh.

Gathering the little *tapi* to take away, they took with feeling their big kisses. *"Bon voyage!"* she said. "You will come and tell me everything when you return." And then they could tell her:

"It's *awful*—taking Boots out there and leaving him alone—"

"Well . . ." And Lily shrugged her shoulders almost the way the doctor had done. "It is where he *belongs*, no? That small one." She actually laughed, and touched the rug again. "We have civilized into some use and some art this tangle of wool, yes? We make order from the thousands of sheeps everywhere."

They made off. Thousands again. Boots was only one to Lily too, and a small one besides.

That night they knelt on their small rugs, side by side. Then they lay listening once more to the muezzin. "I won't be able to bear listening to that—after . . ." Cathy said.

"I *hate* grown-ups!" Pippa said out of the dark. "I'm never going to let them make me like that—*not caring*. All your life they say, 'Don't cry,' 'It doesn't matter.' What I hate most is, 'You'll forget all about it tomorrow.' "

Boots's mournful maaing woke them at dawn. "I'm sure he knows we're going," Cathy said.

"*He* cares," said Pippa.

For a day they did the Tangier Summer Things they had expected to be doing for weeks and weeks. First they went to the Mediterranean beach where thousands of brown bodies lazed in the sun and little waves. Then Mohammed took them to the Atlantic where the waves were pounding and high. High on Cap Spartel they ate a picnic under the lighthouse which was, for people crossing the Atlantic from America, the first sight of Africa. Then they saw the famous Caves of Hercules where ancient inhabitants had cut stones from the walls.

At home again, Mom said, "Ouatif wants you to call her right away."

"Oh, dear, Pippa hasn't time to see everybody."

"She said she promised to tell you when the King was coming."

Even Dad had not known, not *for sure,* as soon as the people. Ouatif said, "He comes tomorrow. They say perhaps the little prince will be with him! People are already going to the streets where they are hanging the flags out."

Tomorrow was a Sunday. "We were going to St. Andrews." Pippa did not say "for the last time"; they had decided not to say the words again, no matter how often they thought them.

"You *are* going," Mum said. "You won't miss anything before noon. Officials here are always hours late for everything."

Mom said, "I wish I had a dollar for every hour I've waited for official affairs to begin."

So they were ushered into St. Andrews to organ music once more, now something slow and sweetly familiar. But they were now seated just behind the new Consul-General who sat where Pippa's father had sat before. Seeing the rather disconcerted look on Pippa's face, Cathy remembered something. Later she told it to Pippa. "When I was little we were having home-leave, between Belgium, I think, and Bangkok. We went to a concert on the Washington Mall and were late because Dad had been at a meeting too long. I said, 'Oh, well, they'll be saving our seats in the front row!' And Dad said, 'Oh, no, they won't! Here at home we find our places along with everybody else.' "

They hurried lunch and then followed the flags that now fluttered from every lamppost, a long stream of red and green. Crowds were waiting, moving restlessly with an excited sound. Cars were not permitted near the route the King would take on his way to the palace on The Mountain. It was fun walking hand and hand through the great feeling of expectancy. Old men in turbans and yellow shoes also walked hand in hand. Berber women, with their red and white skirts looking shining clean, held children on either side and babies on their backs. Small boys ran in gangs, shouting and climbing trees until policemen scolded them down.

"Look at all the soldiers!" Pippa whispered. They were on every corner and in between, some with machine guns and all with pistols swinging. Policemen were on every corner, too, handsome in tan uniforms and white belts and hats and gloves.

"Plenty of Security," said one Foreign Service child to the other.

Time passed. People sat on curbs and Pippa and Cathy sat on a wall by the Spanish School. Water carriers tinkled with bells and sold drinks from goatskins slung over their shoulders. A man with a steaming kettle of soup came along and the soldiers were given bowls and spoons. Babies began to cry for their beds as the sun sank lower and shadows lay eastward across the street. Bands of musicians looked and sounded tired and bedraggled.

"Oh, dear, Boots will be starved," Cathy said. "Do you think the King will really come?"

Then, as dusk fell, a helicopter moved over and a hush fell on everybody but the babies. A roaring was heard, out of sight, and suddenly a fleet of motorcycles came like a prolonged clap of thunder. They passed so swiftly one almost wondered whether they were real.

Then came a stream of huge cars, each one filled with men whose faces passed by rapidly. But then came one car that was open on top, and a ripple of sound began and increased and flags suddenly flew in the hand of every child. Men lifted their sons on their shoulders to see.

"There he is!" "The King!" *"El Rey!" "Le Roi!"* "Hassan!"

He stood with his arms wide. He wore a white fez with a tassel of gold and a long, full, billowing robe of blue. He swept by like a bird. The thunder of the caravan moved swiftly out of sight. How quickly it was over, after the long day. But the people crowding along the avenues were chattering and laughing and shaking hands and kissing each other. It was clear that they were satisfied, that they were saying, "What a great day we have lived today! We have seen history happening. We will always remember. My child will always be able to say, *I have seen the King.*"

"Queen Elizabeth is always on time," Pippa said, "to the minute."

Tom was excited, as pleased as the crowds had been. "Arabs aren't like us," he said. "They're *patient*. They understand Time." And he rushed out again to follow bands of musicians through the streets, marching and dancing with his friends.

Early the next morning the big black car, loaded and ready, left at dawn. Even earlier, with the first streaks of light in the east, Mohammed took the girls and Boots to the Rest Home where he was welcomed and tied to a fence. As Mom had known, they could leave him more easily now to go on to other things for a while. "Soon again! Soon again!" they called back, waving out of the windows.

Then "Soon again!" to Mum, who stood alone calling after them, "Take care!"

Mom and Dad sat up front with Mohammed to begin with; Dad said, as always on a trip, that they would sit "in rotation" from side to side and from front to back. Tom, hung about with camera and binoculars and book-and-map bag, started them off with his most Tom-Tom words: "This trip is going to be an *education*."

Almost at once they were in the country. The villages of Tangier Province seemed familiar now because of the trip with Doctor Prescot, but from a distance they were free of thorns and stones and mud. Animals were everywhere—horses and donkeys along the roads, herds of cows, and yes, flocks and flocks of sheep and goats, every nose down to the grudging July earth.

Cathy thought of Lily's "thousands of sheeps" and of Boots, surely lonely today and miserable among strangers. But she forgot him in her delight at seeing a herd of camels grazing along the road.

Then they drove along the ocean where every town was an old fortress. Asilah, once Portuguese, was having Market Day, and they bought yellow melons from piles higher than their heads. Next Larache, about which Tom found a comment in his guidebook: its fortress was called Kasbah of the Storks. They had to stop for a long lunch with some old army friends of Dad's in the base at Kenitra. Here some American Army Brats took them off to explore an ancient Carthaginian trading post called Mehdia. Ancient Romans had swum where they went swimming, Tom discovered in his book.

"Oh, dear, more official stuff?" Cathy asked in Rabat when they headed for Dad's appointment at the Embassy. She was worried that Pippa would be bored blue.

He promised there would be no more welcoming luncheons except in Imperial Cities—like Rabat and Marrakesh and Fez. Anyway, what did anything matter as long as they were together? Tom-Tom could rattle on with his facts; they had their own secret language. And at night, wherever they stopped, they hung their rugs on the foot of the bed and were instantly at home. And there would be Fez. . . .

Mohammed had been chauffeur for many Consul-Generals and had learned to take them to all the places to go. In Rabat he drove them past the King's palace, set elegantly beyond vast courtyards, and then past earthen battlements that circled the old city. He had come from old Rabat himself and was proud of its hotels, its embassies, its gardens, and the flags flying everywhere. Along the walls flew storks and gulls and pigeons; he was willing to stop while they were fed and admired. "In 1150 Rabat was already a great city," Tom read out, "called Ribat El Fat'h, The Camp of Victory." They looked down on it from the Tower of Hassan.

Dad must play a round of golf with his friends at Dar Es Salam, one of the greatest courses in the world. So they had time to explore old ramparts on the sea, eat at a sidewalk cafe, and visit Rabat's twin city, Salé, on the other side of the river. Next morning they headed south, where Morocco's vast landscapes would alter from ocean to mountain to desert and back again.

Casablanca was a mushroom city with a huge harbor that had been built to serve all Africa. High-rise buildings and lush houses and gardens built for rich businessmen were not what they had come to see. So on to Agadir they went, down the coast. But it was modern too and they found themselves in a splendid Club Mediterranée with an immense swimming pool. "Do you know what the tour book says?" Tom asked in disgust. "This town is known everywhere as the Moroccan Miami!"

Cathy remembered Ouatif's grandmother. "They had a terrible earthquake here and had to build everything brand new," she said.

"I heard a man tell about it," Pippa said. "He came to visit us—he's English, a writer named Robin Maugham and a real poppet. The bed in his hotel *sank* in the middle of the night and he was underground, buried alive for hours and hours. It was all in the *Sunday Times*."

Agadir was in one important way exactly what it had always been—the center for touring the deep south. First they went out to Tiznit, a town of silversmiths. "We could buy our Hands of Fatima here," Cathy said, looking at the beautiful handmade silver pins and earrings and necklaces.

But Pippa looked shocked. "Oh, *no*, Cathy. We must get them in *Fez*—"

Then they went to Tafraout, where they saw black goats climbing high into argan trees to find young shoots to nibble. "Return in the spring," the guide there told Mom who loved flowers, "and I will show you endless almond blossoms."

Best of all was the journey to Goulimine. There were the great camel markets. And all the men riding and selling and buying camels were dressed in blue. Outside the city these men of the desert had pitched tents of black goatskin. "Look, Pippa—their *tattoos!* All in blue!"

Tom brought out a nugget from his old friend, Budgett: "They bought their first blue cloth centuries ago from English pirates. . . ."

Now and then (as in real life, Cathy and Pippa agreed) there were single moments to be remembered forever. Like one dawn when, having arrived at an oasis hotel after dark, they found a new world out of their window. The sun had only just risen and an old man was watering his garden. Rows of green plants alternated with furrows of running water that caught the bronze slant of light. He directed the flow of water with his hoe, like a king directing the rivers of the world. He seemed to grow from the water and earth, his stained pants tucked above his knees, his turban and his beard the same color of gray, striped with black.

"It can't be real—it's a *painting,*" Pippa whispered.

Cathy whispered back, "But a new painting every other minute."

"Yes. And just wait. That's the way it is in Fez." Everything was a preparation for Pippa's Fez.

That whole day was magic. For the first time they saw the sand dunes that went on, as Tom showed them on his map, practically forever. The great Sahara. A shifting marvel, gigantic waves of sand, a frozen red sea rippling in the sun, on and on and on. They took off their shoes and waded in it, slipping and laughing.

"So camels are called Ships of the Desert," Pippa said.

"But they can run fast when they want to. Tom says the Moors call them Drinkers of the Wind."

The next morning they turned north again, toward Marrakesh. On the way to Pippa's Fez beyond. Tom read from his book as they climbed and descended the highest Atlas mountains. "Pliny the Elder wrote about Toubkal—see, there it is! He says it's the most fabulous mountain in all of Africa, as high as Switzerland's Jungfrau. Listen—'Surrounded by sand it lifts up towards heaven, rugged and barren on the side that faces the ocean, covered with thick shade forests and gushing streams on the side facing Africa.' "

He was disgusted that they both preferred the lower plateaus where thousands of sheep were contentedly grazing. But he agreed with them that the most exciting places on the whole trip were the markets everywhere. In villages where piles of melons reminded them of Asilah, they pushed their way through crowds of Berber women and tribesmen. Mom enchantedly bought still lifes of grapes in cunningly woven baskets of leaves, apricots and peaches and purple figs. Beside ripe fields workers sold works of art they had woven of ripe-headed stems of wheat. Finally, in Red

Marrakesh itself, they came to the most fabulous market of them all. Except—always Pippa's refrain—the markets of Fez.

They stayed at the Hotel Mamounia where, Pippa said ecstatically, Winston Churchill always stayed; it was his favorite hotel in all the world. A buggy, looped with flowers and driven by a splendid Moor with a long white beard, took them to the Djema el Fna. He said, smiling, "Here I will wait for you," and they were set free to watch, with crowds of people from everywhere, dancers and acrobats and jugglers and storytellers and snake charmers.

Around the square, small souks sold every sort of food and drink. They had not dreamed olives could come in so many colors. There were piles of dates and Tom remembered from his books that Marrakesh was famous as the date capital of the universe. "Thirty thousand acres of palms were planted in the eleventh century by the founder of the city, a veiled sultan called Yussef Ben Tashfin."

In Marrakesh was more of everything than anywhere else, except (as Pippa remarked of course) in Fez. There were more storks on more and redder walls. More bins spilled over with dried fruits and spices. There were more water-carriers in their fantastic costumes. And the bazaars, as Dad said, were a scavenger's paradise. Certainly they could think of nothing that could not be found there. Masses of buckles and belts and daggers and sheepskins and caftans and hassocks and slippers and bags and jewelry and brassware and candlesticks. Tourist junk lay in piles and hung in loops and strings. Alongside, to be found by those who knew the country, was the finest craft from mountains and deserts.

A row of little shops on one side of the square was especially fascinating to Tom; they were piled with round brown loaves of bread, in three different sizes, set in charming tipsy towers. Selling them were women with colored veils hiding their mouths and noses.

"Look at their *eyes*," Tom said. "Old Budgett says they've learned to make up their eyes better than any other women. Because that's all men are allowed to see." He backed up with his camera. But when he focused and looked up, every single woman had disappeared.

Pippa laughed. Sometimes she really annoyed him with her British air of superiority. "Haven't you read about *that?* They hate to be photographed, especially by a man. They think cameras are the Evil Eye."

Cathy saw that he was nettled to be caught out. But on the road north again he began dishing out wonder-tidbits to make up for it. "There was a sultan called Moulay Ismail who came to power in 1672. He had thirty thousand slaves, twelve thousand horses, a body-guard of seven thousand black Africans, five hundred concubines, and so many wives and children that he said, 'Only Allah can count them.' "

At last they were really headed for Pippa's Fez. Already they had seen so much that even the marvelous gates of Meknès failed to make their mouths fall open. In the mountains nearby was a city called Moulay Idris after the great prophet who had lived and reigned there. Pippa whispered to Cathy, "Do you think we have to stop at Volubilis?"

Tom heard and looked at her aghast. "It's just one of the oldest cities of the Roman Empire!" he said. "And imagine—old Budgett passed it by. But he'd never have missed it if it was really here, the way it is now. He said 'a pile of old Roman stones'—see, they didn't start to excavate it until 1915."

As in all the important places, they were met and conducted about by an official guide. The day was July-hot and Budgett's old pile of Roman stones, built on a flat plain, seemed to gather the heat and throw it back into their faces. Pippa began to droop and lag behind, and Mom watched her anxiously. So far, nobody had been sick on the trip, but she had been watchful, crossing her fingers every day. This precious bundle of Britain must be delivered safely to her Mum back in Tangier, "paying and packing" as Foreign Service women must always do in preparation for the next tour of duty.

"Cathy, what's wrong with Pippa?" Mom asked. "Isn't she feeling well today?"

"She just hates being in crowds of tourists with all these *guides*," Cathy said.

"I thought you two were so interested in archeology."

This particular official guide was one of the best of the whole trip, a pleasant elderly man with thick spectacles who had studied in both England and America. "It is of interest to most of our visitors," he was saying in very good English, "that Volubilis was the first capital of the province, though Pliny the Elder informs us that in the year 80 the Roman procurator had his seat in Tangier."

Old Tangier. That would interest Pippa. But a glance told Cathy that Pippa was not even listening.

"The year *80!*" Tom gazed up at the high decorated columns over his head. "Two *hundred* years ago Washington was at Valley Forge. And two *thousand* years ago, those Roman soldiers were *right here.*"

The guide looked at him approvingly, but Cathy noticed Pippa slip away from the crowd. Maybe she *was* sick. The guide was saying, "In ancient Moroccan history this place was called Tingitan Mauritania . . ."

Mom whispered, "Cathy, do you think it's her stomach?"

"Near here—at Moulay Idris—the history of the Moroccan nation begins. In September, tens of thousands of people come here for the famous Fantasia. This plain and the hills are covered with tents, and our finest horses . . ." Cathy too slipped away. ". . . and the King . . ."

Pippa was sitting on a rock, staring at the ground.

"Pippa—are you all right?" She looked all right. It occurred to Cathy that maybe she was missing her Mum.

But Pippa's voice was quite crisp and cold. "Of course I'm all right. I just hate these empty old *monuments.* They're so *dead.*"

Cathy sat down beside her. "And it's so *hot,*" she said.

"Oh, I don't mind heat, not really, if . . ." Pippa's eyes were suddenly filled with tears as they had been that first time she spoke about Foxy. "I talked to Mohammed—and we are, we're going to Fez at the wrong time, in the wrong direction. We should have come down, by another road. I wanted you to see it the way I did the first time. I told you, remember? At sunset, from the mountain. It was like—" She searched for words. "A huge rose-colored *fungus*." She wiped her eyes. "I thought it was moving, *alive*. And we could hear it, too. I wanted—" She was weeping again. "Oh, I wish we could ever be alone!"

Cathy saw that Mom was coming, looking anxious. She said quickly, "Mom thinks you're sick. Imagine!" She pressed Pippa's arm and turned and ran to Mom, to stop her from coming on. "She's okay. She's just—" How to say it? "She just wanted to see Fez from above—see—on another road."

It sounded petty. But it wasn't. Cathy understood now, completely; but how could she explain? It seemed even pettier when you realized Tom might have chattered on and quoted old Budgett at the very moment, the great special moment Pippa had waited for.

"Really!" Mom was mildly disgusted.

"You see, Fez is terribly important to Pippa—" How to say it? "The very first day she told me how it looked. On the whole trip—it was her most important thing—"

On the way to the car again, Cathy slipped close to Dad and tried to tell him. She saw that Tom was listening. Then Dad called to Mohammed. "Yes, it is so," Mohammed said. "There are many roads, from every direction. Fez is the center—" and Tom got out his biggest map. It would be somwhat longer, but yes, there was a way, a road that went entirely around the city. These long July days sunset was late. . . .

* * *

Not until the car turned northward with the lowering sun on her left did Pippa realize what was happening. Dad pretended to speak quite casually. "We thought it would be a good idea to put Fez against the setting sun."

Cathy had to speak. "See, Pippa, it's going to be *okay*," she said.

Pippa leaned back, staring. A sign said *FEZ 15 K* and she was absolutely stiff and still. The sky to the west was blinding bright, shadows leveling. "Soon," she said to Cathy, and then she cried, "Oh, dear, maybe it was just the way I *felt* that first day! It was the first time I'd really seen *any*thing in Morocco. What if it isn't the same?"

Mom smiled. "But Pippa, it has to be the same." Her voice was gentle. "It's been here more than a thousand years; that's marvelous enough for us!"

Cathy felt a great surge of love for Mom. The sun was only an orange rim, the edge of a great circle of fire. The car made a turn. Mohammed pulled off the road and stopped the engine. There it was.

The ancient city lay in the red and golden light of dusk. The swarm of its medina, its glittering green rooftops and countless minarets were a fabulous embroidery.

"You see what I meant?" Pippa cried. They all walked on the road together, linking hands, looking. "It's as if nobody made it—as if it *grew*."

It seemed to Cathy that the very clouds in the sky had joined a conspiracy for perfection. They changed from red to orange to yellow to mauve. Then, in deepening dusk, Fez began to bloom with little lights.

Tom said the best thing as they got back into the car at last and started for the city itself. "Well, Pippa, now you really seem part of the family."

On the eastern edge of the medina, its back to the hills, was the best hotel in Fez, Palais Jamai. It was once, Tom reported, the house of a Grand Vizier. They were so late that several officials were already waiting in the lobby and protocol began at once. During dinner they all received brochures that told them in large type and bright pictures about the greatest mosques and palaces and universities of Fez.

The girls escaped to their room and presently, clean and cool, they stood on their balcony.

"Listen." Drifting over a sea of moonlit rooftops were the voices of women. A murmur, a laugh, a song. Smoke lingered from supper fires; lamps burned here and there. Somewhere a flute became magic, all by itself; then drums began to beat the exciting rhythms Cathy remembered. "They are dancing now," she whispered, knowing how Moroccan women danced together, and she swayed her hips in her nightgown.

"Do you know what I heard, Cathy? People who know the way can go all over old Fez on the rooftops."

They put their rugs down and knelt on the balcony to watch and to wait for the voices. The first came from a minaret close at hand. And then another—another—another, until they joined together, near and far, from every part of the city. "Tom says he read there was a mosque in Fez for every day in the year." They could believe this as the chanting rose and fell as if, sentence by sentence, it was borne on the warm wind. As the muezzin cried, "Allah!" they spoke to "Our Father," and this was as natural as any other differences between themselves and the women murmuring and moving on the terraces.

"Tomorrow we'll get necklaces for each other on the Street of Silver," Pippa said.

"And wear them forever."

Being in this ancient place made Forever possible. Even likely, as they fell asleep.

Almost at once, it seemed, it was blinding morning, hot by nine o'clock. Plunging into the old medina of Fez was like entering a human anthill. People moved every direction, brushing against each other on streets no wider than alleys. As they walked by twos, following the guide, he suddenly pressed himself against a wall, warning them to do the same.

A cry behind them sounded like *"Baleeeeek!"* It was shouted by an old man with a donkey loaded from its eyes to its tail with boards that narrowly missed the walls on either side. He grinned apologetically as he passed, still shouting. All down the street people plastered themselves to the walls for him or ducked into handy souks. Soon there was another donkey, this time loaded with clanging flat bronze rings that would, the guide said, presently be decorated by the finest engravers.

"I like it," Cathy said as they let this one go ringing by like a bundle of bells. "No machines. Isn't it super?" Having been there before, Pippa was impatient with listening to the guide. She whispered "Smell!" and "Look!" and "Listen!" and "Watch out!" as if she owned it all. And Tom endeared himself to her by obviously preferring her comments to the books and maps in his bag. What was a map worth in this living jungle?

"That smell. What is it?" A strange exciting mixture of spices and oranges and—for a second, dung and donkey—and then mint and fresh-cut cedarwood. Then smoking spiced sausages.

They moved from a hot passage between windowless walls to a cool one shaded by a net of woven reeds. Colors shifted and changed, sunstruck and shadowed.

"See what I meant?"

Mom murmured, "It can't be *true* . . ."

The Bou Inania Medersa, the guide said, was a university built by the Sultan Bou Inane in 1355. They walked on pink marble and onyx pavings in its courtyard between stucco walls and wooden doors massively carved. "It must have taken thousands of workmen donkeys years to do all this," Dad said, and Cathy knew he was thinking "slaves."

Mom said, "Like the great cathedrals."

The guide smiled in a superior way he had and showed them an old clock that had thirteen huge bronze chimes. "Nobody knows now how these are worked, so we believe they were made by a magician in a day. They have been silent now longer than anybody remembers."

"Let's go up ahead," Pippa whispered. They climbed narrow staircases and peeped into rooms where students had lived and worked longer, too, than anyone remembered. On the rooftop they came out over a sunstruck sea of glazed tiles.

"Listen—" The sounds of the living city, shouts, murmuring, tinkling, banging on wood and bronze, donkeys braying. They did not want to go down when the guide beckoned. "Now," he said, "we will visit the Dar Batha—quite new, built by Moulay Hassan in the last century. It is said to be much like the great palaces of Granada."

"A museum," Pippa said, aghast. "It'll take *forever.*"

"Now stay close," Mom said for the tenth time when they were again on the street. When they stopped to splash their hands in a mosaic blue and white fountain she waited. "I would never get used to women looking at me over their veils," she said, "and filling jars with water like the ancient of days."

"Did you know Mark Twain came for a visit to the Arabs?" Tom asked the girls. "He said he wondered why Arab women wore veils—"

"Tom, that's an unpleasant old story that everybody knows," Mom said.

"I don't know it," Pippa said. "I know *Tom Sawyer* and *Huckleberry Finn,* but not about the Arabs."

So Tom finished: "He said when he saw their bare faces, he *knew* why!"

Mom had moved ahead but presently she waited again. "You could get lost in two minutes here," she said. "All of you stay close to the guide and learn something. *He*'s lived here all his life." But it seemed to them he spoke his lines as if they were verses he had memorized.

"This is the best collection of Moroccan weapons.

Men are forbidden to wear jewelry by the Koran, so they decorated their daggers and belts and pistols and powder horns . . . And now you will see the Karaouine mosque—" The guide looked at Mom. "This is often compared to the world's great cathedrals. But unfortunately, only Moslems may enter." They walked around it, glimpsing its wonders through fourteen different doors. "The nave is supported by 270 pillars . . . Twenty thousand worshippers may pray in here together . . . The library of the Karaouine is a center of learning. It has celebrated its eleven hundredth birthday and still sends out—how is it you say?—professors and magistrates—"

"A college of law and education," Dad put it practically. "Impressive."

"And built by a woman," Mom said. "I have done some homework too. Her name was Fatma and her sister Meriem built a mosque and a university just as grand. Isn't that so?"

"It is so," the guide said. He looked rather old and tired by now and was glad to take them to a restaurant for cakes and tea. Tomorrow, he answered Mom's question, they would see the artisans of Fez and the shops.

"There's a special shop—" Pippa began.

The guide spoke to Mom and she said, "He says he knows the best shops where we won't be cheated."

"They never take you to the nice little ones," Pippa said. "The guides work with the huge places, everybody knows that, so they get a cut. But I know a special one where they make things while you're watching—"

Another special Pippa-thing. Mom frowned and Cathy knew she was wondering whether Pippa would be cross again today. Pippa said, "I know exactly where this shop is, from the hotel."

Cathy began to tell this to Mom, but Pippa gave her a quick pinch. "We've got to get away from them," she said. "They'll never let us stop and *look*."

More mosques, museums, tombs. They were glad to sit down for lunch, though it was long and official with everybody talking French. During coffee they escaped and collapsed by the pool.

Her eyes closed against the sun, Pippa lay smiling. "I've got it all figured out," she said. "We can slip out *at dawn*. Nobody will even know."

"By ourselves?" Cathy was alarmed at the notion after the maze she had seen already.

"Who do you want to come along? Tom, telling us what to do?"

"Oh, no—"

"I know exactly where that little shop is, you'll see. That dreary guide would never take us there."

Once more, evening fell with its magic sights and sounds on the terraces. Close at hand, sunset in Fez was marvelous in a different way. It lingered. They lingered. They were both thinking, now we have been here, we have it forever, no matter what, no matter where we go.

Pippa was right. At dawn the lobby was deserted. Even the desk was abandoned, and outside in the court-yard a few figures slept, curled on the stones in their robes with hoods pulled over their faces. But as soon as they entered the huge gate, one of many in the city wall, they found plenty of life. Even so early they had to watch out for the warning *"Baleeeek! Baleeek!"*

"Now we can go just where we want to," Pippa said and began to thread her way expertly among the narrow streets. Cathy took her hand, dizzy with a wild sort of freedom and happiness. They bought some marvelous cakes that came fresh and smoking from a pot of boiling oil. They ate, laughing and licking their fingers. Then they bought a pocketful of fresh-fried almonds and one of fat raisins for nibbling.

Soon several boys were tagging along, begging for shares of everything. A girl said something to two others in a doorway, pointing, and they all burst into giggles. Cathy felt uncomfortable as she had, sometimes, in Tangier. What was it they were saying? What made them laugh?

"It's near here—I remember them hammering on those trays. There's the Street of Bronze and then the Street of Silver." They stood watching a young man hammering intricate designs on a huge tray. Pippa made a sign when he looked up, her hand describing a chain on her neck. But he only grinned and shook his head.

"Anyway, I really know without him," Pippa said. "It was just at the end of this street, to the right—I remember perfectly. I'll just follow my nose."

But such a stink met them on the street to the right that they almost staggered. "Phew!" Cathy cried, "don't let's follow our noses!"

"It's the tanneries. You've simply got to see them—

they're marvelous even if they stink like that, huge pots steaming with hides."

"After we do our shopping," Cathy said, holding her breath.

"We could just nip in a minute, now we're this close." From where they were they could see freshly dyed hides draped everywhere, even on the ramparts above. And there were the steaming vats. Tanners with splashed leather aprons and arms dyed above the elbows waved to them, laughing. They waved back, holding their noses.

"Now which street did we come?" Pippa stopped by a rushing stream that flowed here, under a bridge. "Do you recognize anything we passed?" But no, here were men stitching leather into hassocks. And slippers next. "All we need to do is listen and we'll hear them hammering those trays." But when they followed the clanging of hammers the shop they had seen before was not where it had been. Or had seemed to be. They turned another way. Now the hammering was the gentler sound of carpenters making chests and cabinets. Some of these had tiny shelves behind patterned arches. "Look—this tiny box!" It had a small mirror set beneath a slant of colored tiles. "Like a little house. Let's ask how much—"

A young man who worked on a high bench that almost filled his shop was handsome and dark. *"Cuánto?"* Pippa asked, and he held up five fingers, sending fragrant shavings down the air.

"Five *dirhams.* Too much!" Pippa cried. "Let's pretend to go away," she whispered to Cathy, enjoying herself. "They love bargaining."

"But it isn't much for that pretty—"

"Ssssh! He'll call after us, you'll see, we'll get it for two." To her delight he called after them, "Four!" He was used to English tourists.

"Three!" Pippa said.

They got it for three. He got down and wrapped it in the pages of an old newspaper. Two other young carpenters came from their shops to watch and smile. A crowd of boys pressed in on each side. When they came jauntily to the corner they saw only more and more carpenters ahead, so went back again, the other way. Presently they came to a cross street hung with brilliant caftans; they flew like flags from every shop. "We're getting away from the craft places." Pippa stood uncertain. "Oh dear, we shouldn't have gone off the way we did to the tanneries."

Now they were in a perfect wilderness of clothing souks, silks and embroideries and woolens and blankets. Then they saw more huge boiling pots, but this time along the streets. More men with purple and red and yellow arms, but these were dyers of wool. Over their heads hung huge swatches of threads, dripping colors onto the cobblestones, swinging in a sudden breeze. A dozen, a hundred times as much wool as on Lily's rooftop.

For a little while they forgot everything else in this new enchantment. Everywhere they stopped, now, children gathered around them. They walked between fabric shops with bolt after bolt of material of every kind standing on edge, perfect forests of cloth—cotton, silk, wool—and walls of spools, every size and color. Then came the Street of the Tailors. Inside each shop sat a man sewing edgings on *djellabas* and in front of each stood an apprentice, some very young, briskly crossing threads once every stitch.

"I always wanted to see how they did that," Pippa said. "You see—almost like our buttonhole stitch, isn't it? But how do they do it so *fast?*" A line of donkeys laden with bolts of cloth came trundling along and they had to dodge, with the apprentice, inside the doorway. Dust rose from the brisk hooves of the cheerful little animals and Cathy began to sneeze.

"Now where," she asked, looking and sneezing, "is my handkerchief?" She stopped in dismay. "My purse, Pippa! I've left it—I must have left it at that shop where we got the looking glass."

"Oh, dear," Pippa said. Her eyes went wide. "How *stupid!*" But she did not mean Cathy alone; her own purse was missing too. "Sometimes it slips from my shoulder, but I *always*—"

They walked slowly and soberly, not holding hands or speaking. There was no good going back anywhere. Now they were both very aware of the boys behind them. One sidled closer and called "Cigar-eet?" the way the boys did in Tangier. They walked more briskly. "We were told and *told* to be careful—"

"We'll have to be taken to that shop, after all," Pippa said. Cathy took her hand again.

"Won't Tom *howl* at us getting our purses lost?"

A small boy stopped square in front of them, holding out his hand and looking miserable. He was ragged and his nose was running.

"Let's hurry," Cathy said.

Pippa had stopped; she stood quite still. "Which way is the sun? Can you tell? We should go toward it to get to the hotel—I think." There seemed a kind of diffused haze above them now.

"It seems sort of brighter there," Cathy said, and they turned about. Two of the boys, standing aside but barely, talking in quick loud voices, walked after them. They had to keep walking, no matter what. So they did. Cathy felt hot enough to die, but she didn't say so. She felt ugly little nerves crawling on her legs and arms and wiped her wet forehead with her arm. Suddenly her scarf was snatched from her head. A girl laughed and shrieked when she turned to see—and waving the scarf, disappeared.

"What a horrid girl," Pippa said. There was a word you were supposed to say but she couldn't remember it.

And what horrid boys, they both thought. And horrid streets, crowded and hot. Horrid smells; dung and sweat as the drovers passed, forcing them out of the way again and again.

They walked until they could walk no more. Where were the cool mosques? They saw great closed doors, hung with locks. The sun beat down, but it seemed directly above them now. For a while they crouched by a fountain where women came and went and the boys disappeared. A bearded man spoke to them.

Cathy said eagerly, "We want to go to the Palais Jamais Hotel. Please—" Remembering, she was about to say *s'il vous plaît* but Pippa hissed in her ear, "Don't tell him we're lost!"

The same awful thoughts had begun to go through their minds. Ransoms, kidnappings. The daughter of an

ambassador in South America—a family in Ethiopia—
slaves. The man shrugged, turning away. They walked
again. At the next corner they were sure they saw him
again, watching them. Another man had joined him.

"We've got to ask somebody, Pippa," Cathy said. "I
thought we'd see some tourists and guides, but it's too
hot now—"

Pippa whirled at her. "If you hadn't asked that ugly
man he wouldn't be following us," she said. She kept
walking; Cathy stumbled behind her. "Let's stop and
pretend to look at something, and see if he's still there."
He was, and now two others with him; they talked close
together, their hands on each other's shoulders.

"We could ask a man in a shop—let's ask that man
selling baskets, he looks nice—"

But he only looked blankly at them. Pippa tried
French, Cathy tried her little Spanish. All around them
people were talking the strange and what now seemed
the quite dreadful gutteral talk of Moroccans. The
basket man looked beyond them, uncomfortably. One of
the three men smiled. Once more, the girls fled.

Mom had ordered breakfast for everybody at seven.
The guide was expected at eight. When the girls didn't
appear, Mom called their room; no answer. She went up
and knocked; no answer. A porter unlocked the door so
she could wake them. She called toward the bathroom
over the two rumpled beds. "No breakfast if you don't
get a move on!"

Silence. Nobody. I must have passed them on the
way up, she thought and went down again. No? They
must have decided to take a swim. The pool was empty.

The old garden, of course. Tom went to the roof. When he came back the guide had arrived. A group was assembling, already hot and impatient.

"I had a feeling they were planning something," Tom said. "There was a place that made those Hands of Fatima. They were going to buy them for each other."

"But they'd have better sense than to go into that wilderness alone!" Mom cried.

Dad looked dubious. "Don't get excited," he said, as he always did. "If Pippa knew where the shop was, it isn't a wilderness to her, now is it? Her family stayed here four days last year, remember."

"Do you know where there are shops that have engraved jewelry?" Mom asked the guide.

"Of course, Madam. There are many."

"The minute we go, they'll come," Dad said, cross.

They sat in a small cushioned alcove facing the front door of the lobby. But Mom sat edgily. Dad and Tom talked with the guide about the history of Fez and how it had become a center for Moroccan arts and crafts. "A French writer has called Fez the most magnificent monument to the Moroccan past," the guide said. "But many of the young people do not seem to value this. They go in the evenings to the New Town, dressed like Europeans, without veils or *babouches*. I have seen young girls of the best Fäsi families riding motorbicycles!" He glanced sympathetically at Mom. "They speak of how necessary it is to be free," he said. "Like your daughter and her friend."

"Did they speak of that? Did you hear them?" Mom asked.

"But of course. They must go ahead, like all young

people. They wish to be without guides, without parents . . ." He went to speak to the young man at the desk.

Mom said, "We kept telling them to stay close, didn't we? But did we tell them the reasons? Tom—do you think they understood why they shouldn't go off on their own?"

"*I* did," he said. His look said, "*Girls*—what do *they* understand?"

"Do you think—?"

"I just knew they were planning something crazy."

Mom stood up. "You must go with the guide," she said to Dad. "I'll stay here and wait—if you find them, call me right away." She had turned quite pale. She walked back and forth while he spoke with the guide and the hall porter. "Tom, you stay with me," she said.

He began to protest, but Dad gave him a meaningful look. "Stay and take care of your mother," he said. She went with them to the door and stared after them as they crossed the parking lot and disappeared through the great gate into the maze and swarm of the medina.

"At home, those guards march around the consulate all night," she said. "And all day."

Tom spread his map on the cushions. The medina was a crisscross of markings without names, as haphazard as a bundle of Pick-Up-Sticks. When Mom leaned to look he folded it quickly. No comfort there.

The minutes passed. Half an hour. An hour.

"We should have called the mayor—or is he a governor? Why on earth didn't your father think of it? There are police and soldiers!"

"They'll be back any minute," Tom said. He

sounded exactly like his father and she turned on him angrily.

"We're so *exposed,* all of us, all the time," she said. "It's a terrible life, always among strangers and languages we don't know. And we're always told not to worry, not to be nervous, to trust people and be good examples! No wonder Cathy and Pippa haven't sense enough to be afraid." She was beginning to sniffle and searched desperately in her handbag for a handkerchief.

"Here," Tom said; again just like Dad, he handed her his big one. She walked up and down again, blowing her nose. People looked at her; a crowd of tourists waiting for a bus whispered together. "In just ten more minutes I'm going to call," she said.

But in five minutes, Dad appeared. *He* had called. And they heard the curious repeated wailing of police cars. In the courtyard the Chief of Police asked questions. Mom had to go upstairs to look at what was there before she could tell them what the girls were wearing. Sundresses, by Moroccan standards for girls as big as they, were distressingly naked. She realized that now. All very well in a crowd, but now the idea of them wandering half-naked in the souks!

"What do you think, for heaven's sakes," Dad asked her, "that they're being sold in the slave market for somebody's harem?" He meant it to be funny, but it wasn't.

"There *is* a marriage market, I read about it the other day," Tom said, unhelpfully. Dad glared at him. Now everything that had seemed interesting and exotic had become strange and sinister.

"I'm going with the Chief," he said. "They're probably just wandering around looking at shops and things. They're so silly—they've no idea of time when they're together."

"Can't I go?" Tom barely got the words out when Dad's look stopped him.

Mom walked back and forth again, like a tragic queen in an old play. An American tourist came and asked Tom a question. Anyway, he was taking care of his mother. That was important, after all. Mom might look like a distracted old bird but he, his shoulders square and his head high, was the one in charge of this theater of operations.

"Let's just sit in this restaurant until they go away," Pippa whispered. It was really only a small bar, with three rickety tables against a wall. Young men drinking coffee at two of them looked at them frankly. One said something, obviously clever, and they all laughed. Uncomfortably, as she had many times before in every country she ever went to, Cathy wondered, "What are they saying?" Tom said he gathered from his friends that all Moroccan men thought all women were weak and silly.

"Shall I face the door—or shall you?" Pippa asked.

Nervous because of all those eyes, Cathy giggled and said, "We could flip a coin—if we had one!" But it was not an amusing thought just now. Without money, they could not even order anything. She suddenly thought of the royal and careless way she had parked Boots for ten franc pieces. And she recalled uncomfortably the many hands held out to her and to Dad and

Mom and Tom on their travels, hands empty and asking.

But Pippa said, "They don't know we haven't any money. So we'll just order and sit here—just sit and *sit* until somebody comes. They have to be looking for us by now."

"Mom'll be frantic," Cathy said. "I'll face the street, Pippa—we can take turns watching."

Pippa ordered two mint teas in her confident school French. Then, in the ominous stage-whisper they had both begun to use the last half hour, she said, "Remember how long people sit at the cafés in the Socco in Tangier? Hours over *one glass*—" They both remembered how much fun it had been to sit there, cozy at a small table like this one, watching the world go by. But now Cathy had to report that the three men had passed, had come back, and were standing there smoking. She picked up the glass the waiter brought. "Take tiny sips," Pippa said. "What are they doing now?" Her eyes looked huge and scared over her glass.

"Just standing, looking."

Two men at a table behind them paid the waiter, got up and went out into the street. Two of the men in the doorway came in and took their places; the other stood by them, leaning against the wall.

Cathy choked. "Don't drink so fast," Pippa said. "Look, yours is half gone."

They might be bandits from the Sahara, Cathy thought. In her mind she went trundling off, swathed in hot veils, on a camel. "I wish we'd just stayed in Tangier," she said. "We could have gone riding every day. And we could have seen Boots every day. Even if our medina isn't as big, it's lovely. Isn't it?"

Pippa sounded forlorn. "I like the sea much better than I do mountains." The Mediterranean lay cool and blue in their minds and Atlantic whitecaps rolled splendidly over their fear. Neither said the most important thing: in Tangier they knew their way, they knew the nice men in the *bacals,* in the cafés. Everybody knew who they were and where they lived. They were guarded and safe.

"But we loved the trip until now," Cathy said. They changed places and it was Pippa's turn to stare. "What are they doing now?"

"They're getting orange squash."

"Even if somebody passed they wouldn't see us— shouldn't we stand on the street again?"

"We can't go out, remember? We can't *pay!*"

They sat silent, taking the tiniest sips they had ever taken in all their lives. Pippa crumbled another sugar lump into tea that was too sweet already. "This absolutely *gags* me," she said.

"Mom likes tea without any sugar at all, but she says nobody in all Morocco will believe it." The thought of Mom caused a sharp pain in her stomach. "She always gets a stomachache when she's nervous."

"Mum gets a headache." Pippa gazed at Cathy over the rim of her glass. "So do I," she said.

The Arabic gutterals all around them seemed strange and fierce, even the waiter's "Barakalofic" to another departing customer.

They did not know, of course, that at that very moment Mom was in the Ladies' Lounge having a terrible stomachache. Dad found Tom waiting outside the door. One look at his face and Tom knew there was no use asking whether the girls had been found. Dad knew too, but he asked anyway, "They haven't come back here then? I thought I'd better come and check."

"No. And Mom's sick—"

Dad sat down. "Why don't you go with the men now, and I'll stay with her for a while," he said.

Tom leaped up. The guide stood looking nervous. "Did you look into the cafés?" Tom asked. "I was just thinking. What they'll do is go into some café when they get too hot and tired. That's what I'd do."

"We tried all the jewelry shops. They hadn't been near one of them," Dad said. "The police talked to some men who had seen them earlier. They apparently bought a looking glass."

Tom grinned. "That was them, all right," he said.

"And somebody said they had their purses snatched."

"*No—*"

"I'm not telling your mother about that," Dad said. "Wait here a minute while I get another check cashed." He went to the desk and then gave Tom a manly slap on the shoulder and slipped a small roll of bills into his hand. "If you think somebody might sell some information—" he said in a low voice. "The guide says he knows somebody who has done this sort of thing before. The police were looking for him."

Their eyes met. In a couple of years, Dad thought, noticing how tall Tom was beside the guide, he might actually have to look up at Tom. He went back and asked a woman if she would please go into the Ladies' Lounge and find out how his wife was feeling.

She hurried. And almost at once out came Mom, pale and ill-looking. "You didn't find them yet? Do you think we should call Pippa's mother?" To be so *responsible;* now it frightened her. "Or alert the British office here?'

"Not yet," he said.

"What are they doing now?" Pippa whispered.

"Smoking more cigarettes. Except one. He has one of those long clay pipes—"

"*Kif!*" Pippa said. "They're drug addicts, that's why they're desperate for money." It was as if they had stepped into the leading parts in some weird TV show. They stared at each other. After all, three governments would be involved; it would be headlined in every newscast all over the world. Like that poor vet's family in Ethiopia.

Cathy whispered, "Another one is getting his pipe filled. Don't you think—" Her voice was shaking. "While they're just sitting there, we could suddenly *run*—"

"Oh, no, they'd shoot. If they saw us getting away. Anyway, the waiter would yell, he'd think we were trying to get out of paying for our tea."

"All we can do is wait." Now there was nothing left in either glass. A second waiter came to take the glasses and laid a small white slip on the table. Cathy saw that the first waiter was talking and laughing with the kidnappers; they all looked toward the girls, obviously talking about them. "The waiter is with them now," she said, leaning over the terrible white bill they couldn't pay. "They're all looking—"

The new waiter stood awkwardly with the two empty glasses, waiting for the money. He was very young, only a boy really. Pippa said in French, "Two more teas, please." He only looked puzzled. So this one spoke no French.

"Oh, dear," Cathy said, looking up at his uncertain face. He smiled and walked over to the older waiter and spoke to him. All of them looked at the two girls. One of the men at the table got up, holding his long red pipe in his hand and moved to their table. They sat frozen as he picked up the bill. His voice was quite kind; he spoke in hesitating English: "It is one dirham fifty; each tea is seventy-five francs."

Cathy had an inspiration. "We have no money with us," she said clearly. "We are waiting for my father. He is coming soon. While we are waiting we would like two more glasses of tea." She met Pippa's admiring eyes. They had bought a little more time. He spoke to the waiter and then, to their horror, drew up a chair and began to ask questions, leaning back and puffing at his long red pipe.

Dad said to Mom, "Please, darling, don't be silly. They have simply forgotten the time. They forgot the time every day at home and we never worried. Things like that don't happen."

Mom said, "They *do* happen! All the time. You

know it and you're as frightened as I am."

"I'm not frightened," he said, "but I *am* angry, I'll tell you that much. Now we'll never make Midelt tonight—our whole schedule is out."

She gave him a withering look. "You talk about keeping schedules when your daughter may be in danger. That was the trouble in the first place. They were bored with your schedules—they couldn't do anything they really wanted to do because you had to see all these people wherever we go. That's the way it is with you so-called Public Servants all the time!"

"Wait a minute!" Dad said. Now and then, ever since they had begun to travel from place to place and home to home every few years, Mom had these moments of blaming everything on his "career."

"It's true!" she cried. And her tension had become by now so extreme that she began to tremble and cry. "Children need security, something to be the same for at least a little while. Cathy can't have a pet or a friend or even a home of her own!"

It was quite hopeless to reason with her, he could see that. The thing he had learned to do with her in this mood, and with Cathy as well, was to let her talk it out or cry it out. No good reminding her just now that she had helped him decide on a Foreign Service career, that she had been happy and romantic about living in new exotic places and idealistic about getting "to know and understand the world." If he reminded her just now that they had agreed their children should be Citizens of the World, she might only cry harder. She would remember that all Cathy wanted was One Good Friend. She would say, "Who can learn Spanish and then

French and Flemish at the same time and then Siamese or whatever they talked in Thailand, with only two years for each and these years busy with Cultural Exchanges." He only said, "Sit down, darling. I've ordered a cup of tea," and gave her his handkerchief and held her hand.

Tom looked up at the policeman at his side. "If we were in New York—see, they search every street—hundreds of them on motorcycles and in police cars." But he could see that even one motorcycle would never do in a narrow Fez street. If it started out it would mow down kids and donkeys and carts and women before it had gone a hundred yards. "Here, I can see it's rather like looking for a needle in a haystack."

The policeman smiled and Tom knew that he had no idea what a needle was, or a haystack either. He was beginning to realize how confused and frightened those dumb girls must be by now. As the group of policemen marched along they held their hands on their pistols and looked right and left, up and down, pushing those who failed to vanish into doorways out of the way. The strangeness of the city really struck Tom. A huge web, its alleys like dirty threads between windowless walls.

For the first time his mind began playing tricks on him—he saw those silly things crouching in a tiny room without windows; chased like people in a spy film over the rooftops . . . He shook himself and looked up for the blue that had to be the sky. For just a stupid second, he imagined those two being auctioned off for brides to a turbaned sheik in a slave market—

But actually they were at that moment sitting paralyzed at a small round table.

"You are Americain?" the Arab asked in a polite soft voice.

"Yes," Cathy said. "My father—" She felt Pippa kick her under the table and flushed. She must not, of course, let him know that their fathers were important or he would know they would make excellent hostages. "He is buying bread for our lunch," she said, trying to look sad and poor like the beggar children who sometimes stopped them on the streets in Tangier.

"He returns here?" the man asked.

"With his friends," Pippa said quickly. "With our *group.*" He must think there would be too many to be easily overpowered.

"Fez ver-ee complicate. I thought perhaps you had lost the way," he said. "I thought, when your tea had finish, I could show you the way to your hotel. Jamais Palais, no? Yesterday I saw you there." Was he laughing at them now? Certainly he knew that poor people did not stay at the Jamais Palais.

He had probably followed them ever since they left the hotel at dawn. He knew about their purses. He knew they were probably lying and not expecting anybody. He made a little bow, said something that sounded like, "May Fez be kind to you," and returned to his table.

They sat staring silently at their tea. Cathy stirred her spoon among the drowned green leaves. She noticed that her hand trembled like her great-grandmother's who insisted on pouring tea from her own pot until the day she died.

"We mustn't move," she said, as if talking to her

own fingers, but Pippa knew what she meant.

"Cathy, it's all my fault," Pippa said. "From the very first time we talked about a trip, I wanted to show you Fez. I thought it was the most marvelous sight in the world."

"I know." Their eyes met. Even the particular first view from the mountains the very same sunset hour. That was only the night before last; but now it seemed a long time ago.

"You were right. I can see how you felt. I don't blame you at all."

"I was so determined to show you by myself," Pippa went on miserably. "I said I knew that shop was just around the corner, but it wasn't true. I knew that horrible old guide would take us to a huge expensive shop—he'd never give us time to look for the little one."

Cathy said nothing, but reached out and touched Pippa's hand, which was trembling too. She had loved Pippa's idea of the necklaces from the first day. The way she loved the prayer rug. Those two things had become the only two things of each other they could hope to keep.

"So I figured out just when we could get away,' Pippa said. "I was sure that if we went up and down that very first street we would find that shop. And then— we could just turn around, facing the sun, and come back to the gate by the hotel." As Pippa spoke, the ordinary sound of the city, the rumbling-clattering-murmuring-shouting that blends all together so that one almost ceases to hear because it never stops, was suddenly overhung by a voice from a nearby tower. First that voice, then two more, than voices from every direction.

Cathy's eyes lifted and met Pippa's and they knew together. The people near the door, the men at the tables, the boy setting his tray down upon the counter— they all moved as if a giant swivel turned them. East. Meeting, their eyes told each other: *East*.

They stood up and moved, their hands tight together, toward the door. On the street they had only to look which way all the people were facing. The great voices went on. They walked steadily, easily, without a doubt. Before the voices ceased and the people rose, turned, went about their business, they were walking out of the medina under the great gate.

They were as eager to arrive home now as they had been to leave it. Even stopping for the last lunch at beautiful old Chauen seemed more delay than they could bear. But once more there were people Dad must see, young people in the Peace Corp who were bringing power and running water to this high mountain village.

Tom noticed that the signposts sometimes said Chaouén and sometimes Xauen. "Budgett says they're both wrong," he said. "The right way is *Chef*chauen." Waiting for Dad and Mom they walked through a market that would have seemed splendid before Marrakesh and Fez. The red walls of an old fort, pocked with swallows' nests (and bullets, Tom said) were great for tourists who could get no farther into the wonders of Morocco.

They walked up steep village streets. A familiar thumping and they saw men weaving at looms almost as big as the rooms they worked in. It was a town of high walls, built along steep steps and streets paved with stones shiny and slick from centuries of people and animals walking over them. Many of the houses were painted blue, dark and sky-color splashed on whitewashed plaster. Over the years it had been dripped on walls and stones, layered on it like frosting on a cake. In its own way, this was as strange as anything they had seen. Again and again they had to stand aside for donkeys laden with jars of water—or milk? or honey?—and baskets of sticks and stones.

A boy nudged Tom, holding out his hand and murmuring. Tom shook his head and said "Nada—nothing," and turned out empty pockets. Then the boy put three fingers to his mouth and puffed. "Cigareet?" No, Tom said, he did not smoke. Then the boy nudged again and said "Me guide! Good! Spik Inglis."

Just like Tangier.

At last on the road again, it became more and more familiar. Cathy and Pippa whispered together and Cathy touched Mohammed's shoulder. "Could we turn off on the old airport road?" They were, as Tom said, doing a kind of Fez-thing about Tangier; they wanted the familiar first view. When it appeared they sat tense and silent. On the last curve Cathy said, "It's not too late to ride today, is it, Mom? We could go and see Boots."

"He'll have gained weight while we were gone,"

Pippa said. And suddenly, "Cathy, you'll go on making those reports, won't you?" Once again, now everything was "The Last."

"I imagine," Mom said, "Pippa will want a visit with her mother first—" and the car turned into the big black gates.

As if she had been watching, Pippa's Mum came rushing out, and Mom said fervently, "Well, here we are, all safe and sound."

Cathy and Pippa stood staring behind her. Out of the door came the last of the welcoming committee. The International Lambs. Each of them held a flag. The Union Jack. The Stars and Stripes. And the Moroccan red with its green star. Rajah was the one to make a speech. They had arranged a special meeting at her house, as a hail and farewell to their honorary member.

Mom and Mum and Dad and even Mohammed joined in a big *Maaaaaaaaa*—and in a Hurrah, a Halla-lujah, and a Hamdulah.

They cycled to the stables. The stableman let them saddle the horses. He seemed to know they did not feel like talking and only waved as they cantered off. Past the pet cemetery, through the river, and there was the Rest Home meadow. They saw the flock grazing on the other side and tried to pick Boots out. "Let's call him," Cathy said. "Boots! Boots!" Pippa joined her. But the little flock paid no attention.

"He's not used to us on horses," Cathy said. They got down and tied the horses to a post. "Let's walk closer and then call. I used to whistle when I came home from school."

They called. She whistled. The noses of the flock kept stubbornly to the ground. From this distance there seemed to be many sheep Boots' size, their legs were lost among weeds. From the door of the barn Allal emerged, smiling. He had a little cane flute in his hand, which he waved at them. "He will come!" he called. And looking like an aging Pan at this distance, he began to play a high sweet tune.

Pippa and Cathy stood still by the fence. All the sheep had lifted their heads and now, slowly, began to walk toward them. Coming nearer, they moved faster. And now they saw Boots, recognized him at the same moment. Allal opened a wire gate and took hold of him.

They ran to him, holding hands. Boots stood looking at them. He looked like all the other sheep they had seen everywhere, his wool rusty and stained, the color of the road. It lay in clumps on his back. They knelt on either side and began to run their hands through his coat, not looking at each other. Burrs and bits of seed were caught in it.

"He's probably got ticks all over," Cathy said.

Allal stood smiling. He had closed the gate against the other sheep. "You will take him away now?" He glanced, puzzled, toward the horses.

"No. Today we only came to see him. We brought him a present." They had found a pretty collar in a Berber village where leatherwork had been especially fine. Dangling on it was a small hand they had fastened with a chain. They began to put it around his neck, but he kept turning his head impatiently.

"This is a fine collar. Here it will be lost. Boys will

take it away," Allal said. And it looked quite unsuitable, they had to agree. They looked at each other. Another time, when he was clean, when he was himself again. Cathy unfastened it and stood up. Pippa stood up too. Boots turned abruptly and started for the gate which Allal had opened again for him. He paused, looked back and made a loud *baaa*, then trotted off. Paused again. Then he put his nose to the ground and began to graze like the others.

"Did you hear Rajah say how many new lambs they have every spring?" Cathy asked when they were mounted again. Her voice broke off. As if any lamb could ever be the same!

The two horses knew the path. Up their favorite hill, walking together. Most of the flowers were gone now; only small purple thistles were blooming. But the pines were green and eucalyptus trembled in the usual Tangier breeze. They began to lope on a path shaded and brown and sweet-smelling. And presently, opening like all the world and time, they saw the sea.

"Let's walk them for a while," Pippa called.

Side by side, they were silent. Then Pippa said, "Everything seems sort of—well, sort of odd and different today. You know what I mean?"

Cathy knew.

"It was horrid seeing Boots like that," Pippa said. She leaned forward to touch Habibi's shining mane. "I can't bear to think these horses will get old like Brandy and Soda."

Something stood between them, a truth they did not want to know. And Boots—he would not be stabbed in the throat like the rams of Aid el Kabir—Dr. Prescot would see to that. But changing, separating, these were sure to happen.

"I wish—" Cathy stopped. She was not sure what she had meant to say.

Presently they dismounted to rest the horses and to enjoy the vast view of ocean, forest, mountain, and the white city looking small and remote.

Pippa said, looking far off, "Dad says the minarets in Turkey are super—really different from the ones here. I'll tell you. And send some pictures right away."

But they both knew telling and pictures didn't help much. There were sounds, smells, the feel of places. Cathy thought of the golden gods in Bangkok and barges on the klongs and weavers with heaven knew how many silk threads in a warp. And they both thought of Fez.

At last Pippa said, "Remember that day in Volubilis? So hot and dead. I absolutely and forever knew, that day, I'd never be an archeologist."

"And Dr. Prescot mucking around with his long rubber gloves. . . ."

They could reach each other's minds now. Why not?

"Women get to do all sorts of things in the State Department now," Cathy said. "They're not just secretaries any more. Consuls. Even ambassadors."

"We'd be near enough, sometimes, for visits."

"We might even be in the same place at the same time again. Who knows?"

"Anyway, there are long leaves. We'll be making piles of money, you know. We can fly anywhere."

"By the time we're through college, planes will be going a thousand miles an hour."

They mounted again. "Let's have a real ride now," Pippa said. "They'll really run on the way home."

Cathy sat still for a moment, watching her start down the road.

"Come on, you poke," Pippa called back. "Let's go!"